SPELLBOUND SEDUCTION

A WIZARD LOVE STORY

G.M. FAIRY

To all the good girls who yearn to play with fire.

CONTENT WARNING

For a full list of content warnings in this book, please go to my Instagram @g.m.fairyauthor and check the Google Docs in the link in my bio.

PLEASE NOTE

This book can be read as a standalone or as the third part of a three-book series. To get a better understanding of Winston, Beck, Liona, G.M. Fairy, and Happily Ever Endings, read *Get In My Swamp: An Ogre Love Story* and *Stay In My Swamp: An Ogre Happily Ever After*.

CHAPTER ONE

WINSTON

The buzzing fluorescent lights overhead scratch at my pounding headache. It's nine in the morning on a Saturday. As manager and co-owner of a new club in the magical community, sleep is a luxury I can't afford.

Light pools in from the tall windows overhead, and it's unnerving to see Happily Ever Endings in the light of day. The clean-up crew always does a good job, but I know what happened last night—nothing *clean* transpired here.

I walk through the main floor, looking over the bar countertops, the chairs, and the couches to ensure everything is spotless. I've always paid special attention to detail, but tonight, it's crucial that everything is perfect. The club's franchise owner, G.M. Fairy, is making an appearance.

Although she has been here before, she has not seen the place in full swing. Even though the club has been doing well for the past three months, I want to impress her with a packed house and a steady stream of money. I want to ensure she fully believes that tasking myself and the other co-owners, Beck and Liona, to open this branch in our tiny magical community was her greatest business venture. This club means more to me than anything else in my life, and I plan to keep it for as long as I can.

I walk onto the main stage and look out at the surrounding chairs and couches, frowning once I notice a few red velvet seats in the first row aren't straight. I snap my fingers, and the chairs turn and face me fully. That's better.

I pace the stage, looking around to ensure there are no signs of marks on the glossy hardwood floor. Last night, we had a guest performer, a minotaur, and his milking mistress grace the stage. Let's just say it was a bit of a mess, and I want to ensure there's no sign of it. It's a fresh start to a new day and that means new entanglements to clean up later. Everything is perfect, though, just as it always is.

I'm about to hop off the stage and check to see if we're fully stocked behind the bar when I take one last look at the non-existent crowd. My heart beats just a bit faster, imagining what it would be like to perform on this stage. I shake my head and hop off. I can't let myself think of such things. It would never be possible for me to perform or even be intimate in private. There's no need to torture myself with impossible wishes and dreams.

After checking over the bar and ensuring everything is stocked—except those damned Gumdrop Buttons, hopefully, Liona could get in a shipment before tonight—I return to my office.

I wave my hand, and the door shuts behind me. I don't remember leaving my office in such disarray, but papers and old coffee mugs are scattered across my desk. I shake my head, disappointed at myself for leaving a mess to clean up today. I grab papers and try my best to organize them in cohesive piles. Then, I remember that I'm a wizard and don't need to lift a finger.

My mother always made it a point that I learned to care for myself without magic. "Of course, I hope you'll be so powerful one day you won't have to do anything for yourself, but you should do the manual work whenever you can. We're humans first, wizards second. Life goes by too fast if we don't spend time on the little things."

She's no longer around to drill this message into me, but even as a grown man, I honor her wishes whenever possible. Besides, I think she was on to something with that sentiment.

As I fidget with the articles on my desk, my reflection catches my attention in the mirror across from me. Man, I look like shit. My curly brown hair is a disheveled mess, dark circles shade my blue eyes encasing them, and my skin is a lifeless color. Maybe today is a good day to use my magic to make my life easier. I think Mother would agree that running on only three hours of sleep is a good enough excuse to take a shortcut.

I open my desk door to retrieve my wand. This is just my office wand. It's not as sophisticated as the one I keep at home, but it will do with such a trivial task as cleaning up my office. I flick the wand over my desk, and the papers and mugs travel to their proper position or disappear.

Nothing feels better than working in an organized space. I breathe out once I sit behind my desk, my head whirling with everything I must do today before G.M. arrives.

I could call Liona and Beck for help. They're not only my co-owners but also my best friends. We're probably too close for platonic best friends—I've seen them in their most vulnerable moments and enjoyed every second of it, but I guess that's the kind of friendship you get when hanging out with people who run a magical sex club.

I've never been one to ask for help; in fact, people usually come to me when they're in a bind.

Besides, Liona and Beck just had a baby. They married a few months ago and are in marital new family bliss. They're as happy and distracted as an ogre and human in love could be. I can't bother them with tedious paperwork and ordering. Tonight's their first night back in the club anyway. They should be eased back into everything.

"I know!" I tell myself before rummaging in the other desk drawer until I find the dusty vial of blue liquid. It's an energy potion I made back in college. I haven't needed it in years, but today is the day to try it again. I bring it to my lips and gulp the contents in one chug. Black spots cloud my vision, and my head pounds. It only lasts a few moments, though, and then it's like electricity runs through my brain. It won't last long, five hours at most, and will make me feel hyperemotional and sensitive, but it's worth it if I can just get through all this payroll paperwork. Tonight will feel different. Even after the potion has worn off, the energy from the people and the events will bring me back to life. They always do. That's why I love what I do.

***

"Winston, darling, it's so good to see you." G.M. Fairy flutters over to me and air kisses both sides of my cheek. She's an older fairy godmother, but she has a refined beauty. The low lights catch on her bejeweled red dress. Tall trolls flank both sides of her, their expressions hidden by their dark shades, but I know she even has more people behind them. She always comes with a crew.

G.M. Fairy is a powerful woman. Not only is she a master of her craft in creating potions and spells, but she also owns one of the most successful magical sex clubs. And now she is the franchise owner of the second most successful magical sex club, this one. At least, I'm predicting that's our ranking. I've frequented a few around the United States, and none hold a candle to Happily Ever Endings.

I've been at the club for ten hours today, but after a quick shower and another shot of the energy potion, I'm feeling a hell of a lot better than I did a few minutes ago.

"You look ravishing as always, Ms. Fairy." I kiss her hand delicately.

"That's why I love you, Winston. You're always a devilish flirt. How's everything going?"

I turn toward the club. "See for yourself." The night is in full swing. The music is a low growl. The lights are dim but bright enough to reveal the most intimate scenes. It's packed; creatures of all sorts walk around or lounge on every surface. The performance on the main stage—a solo act with one of the community's sirens.

I thought it was a stupid idea when G.M. Fairy proposed opening this club here in the magical community. Our community was small, with only about three thousand occupants. I wasn't even sure if most would be interested in something like this. But G.M. assured me that creatures would come from near and far, and she thought our community had a little more spunk than I thought. She was right. There were people I knew my whole life who I never even thought had sex that were regulars. It was a community hit and a frequent stop for all magical creatures visiting the Florida area. Sure, we had to figure out some border control issues. Still, it didn't take long for me to develop a spell that only allowed magical beings into the community to keep our whereabouts a secret from non-magical folks.

The club has given me a new purpose and makes me feel part of something greater. It also helps satisfy my most primal needs. The ones I can't satisfy on my own. No, it hasn't got rid of the longing I know I'll never be able to extinguish, but it keeps those needs at bay.

G.M. nods as she looks around. "Everything looks fabulous! Great job, Winston. Are Liona and Beck here?"

"Yes. They're just getting ready for their performance."

"Ah, I can't wait to see. I hear that after a baby, everything is heightened. I want to talk to them before they go on."

"Yes, of course. I'll take you to them." I begin to lead the way, but she stops me.

"Actually, there's something we need to address first. I brought someone for you."

"For me?" I look back at her, the crowd behind her, still unable to see much due to the towering trolls.

"Yes, I figured that you might help her. She has a condition similar to yours, well, sort of."

G.M. Fairy is one of the only people who know the real me. That's how we met so many years ago. I went to her to seek help. Unfortunately, she couldn't do much, but I've learned how to live through it, and for now, that's enough.

"Marigold, darling, come here," she calls back to her entourage.

The crowd parts, and a small woman walks through them.

My heart stops.

I've always been keen on the beauty around me. I've never been one to deny myself the simple pleasure of gazing upon a beautiful woman, but this feeling rushing through me is different. My flood of emotions could be the energy potion finally making me crash, but I know it's not that. Whatever is happening is much, much worse.

Marigold walks next to G.M., her face hung low. She's wearing white silk gloves. I can imagine why.

"Marigold, I'd like to introduce you to Winston."

She looks up at me, and if I thought my world stopped before, I was gravely mistaken. Her hazel eyes seem to take inventory of every piece of me. She tucks a strand of her golden blonde hair behind her ear. Her cheeks heat when she catches my stare and hurriedly returns her gaze to the floor.

The disappearance of her gaze on me feels like the air has been taken from my lungs. I want to grab her face and demand she return her eyes to me, but I don't. I just bow. "It's a pleasure to meet you, Marigold." I don't reach to take her hand. I knew that wouldn't be a good idea. But every cell in my body begs to touch her, to grab her, and never let go.

And then the realization of G.M. Fairy's words ring through me, "*She has a condition similar to yours,*" and a weight falls on my chest. She can never be mine—never be in my arms. I've known her for two seconds, but it's enough. These two seconds are all it takes for the girl I can never have to consume all of me.

CHAPTER TWO

MARIGOLD

What am I doing in this place? My inner dialogue repeats the exact phrase as if it's a blaring alarm warning me to run.

I knew that G.M. wasn't just a magical fairy that made all your dreams come true. I knew she owned a sex club, even if I didn't realize what that entailed. She said we'd be visiting another sex club owned by a wizard who could help me, but I didn't expect it to be like this. Or I did, I'm not sure. But thinking about a sex club and actually standing in one are two entirely different things.

Low and sensual music blares all around me. People and creatures, barely wearing any clothing, slink throughout the space, giving me longing looks. Moans of pleasure come from a distance, but they're not distant enough. My heart races, and I'm unsure if it's from terror or excitement. I've never experienced anything like this before.

I'd barely been out of my hometown of Las Vegas in my nineteen years. Now, here I am, on the opposite side of the country, in a sex club in a magical community. My father would have a heart attack if he knew I was here—except that would be impossible. The thought of my father comes so naturally, and the realization that he isn't alive anymore slams into my chest immediately after. When will his death get easier? Probably never. I don't deserve to have any relief.

Winston, the owner of this place, can't keep his steely blue eyes off me. G.M. only introduced us seconds ago, but he stares intently at me as if he wants to burrow inside and never leave. It's hard to ignore the constant looks from everyone who's passed me by since I entered this place, but his feels different. I stare at the floor, not wanting to catch his gaze, but I can feel it like a lump of searing coal trying to make its way into the most fragile and vulnerable parts of me.

"Let's talk in my office." He says to G.M. This is the second time I've heard his voice, and it still makes my knees wobble.

"Yes, lead the way," G.M. replies.

I'm unsure if I want to be in a small space with this man, even if G.M. is with me. But I guess it's better than standing in this sex dungeon, feeling like anyone could devour me at any second.

I follow behind G.M., who's floating behind Winston. Her trolls stay close behind, but the rest of the entourage we arrived here with is long gone—dispersed amongst the sin and darkness.

We're led to oak doors at the far end of the club, similar to where G.M.'s office is situated in her club.

Winston leans against the door, his arm outstretched as he ushers G.M. and me to enter, but when I pass, he seems to take up more space like he wants me to rub against him. I can't tell if he's trying to intimidate me or daring me to touch him. G.M. said that he had a condition similar to mine. Surely, he must know I can't touch him, but the look in his eyes tells a different story.

Technically, people can touch me as long as it's my clothing and not my skin, but still, I wouldn't say I like to test it. I wear a gown and gloves covering every inch of my body except my neck and face, but I'm still nervous that something might tear or that my powers have gotten stronger and would seep through the fabric. I've never gotten the chance to see the strength of my curse. Well, except the once, which was enough to terrify me for the rest of my life.

I can't bring my gaze away from him this time. The shape of his angular jaw, the way his brown wavy hair frames his face—it's almost impossible not to stare. His attention is so focused on me that it's as if I'm the only being in this world.

My body tingles, and my lungs constrict as if they forgot how to inhale. Maybe this is a trick. He is a powerful wizard, and I've never felt this way before. G.M. might be wrong about him. Maybe he doesn't want to help me. Maybe he wants to ruin me. At least, that's all I can see in his eyes.

I suck in a breath and muster up all my courage, steeling my gaze to the office before me and walking past him. If he wants to play with fire, so be it. I feel his heat as I pass, but that's all I feel. I've made it safe inside without touching him, luckily for him. But I can't deny how my body longs to try again, to experience what it would feel like to brush against that hard chest—the evidence of it under his tight black button-down shirt—as fucked up as that is.

The office is warm and cozy, nothing like the club we were just in. All the walls have dark wood paneling matching the flooring. He's decorated the space with muted oriental rugs and scenic oil paintings, giving the office a homey feel.

"Have a seat." His voice surprises me again. It's like it's made of silk and fire and can seep deep into my veins. I want to bathe in it.

God, what is wrong with me? It must be something about this place. It is a magical sex club, after all. It wouldn't be hard to believe that you're put under a spell as soon as you walk through the door. It would be good for business.

Or it could just be him. He alone would be good for business.

I take a seat in the leather wingback chair next to G.M. Fairy.

"Can I offer you two a drink?" He asks from behind us. The clinking of glass must mean he's already pouring himself something.

"Yes, dear. You know what I like. Scotch on the rocks," G.M. replies.

It's silent for a moment.

"Marigold?" My name has never sounded so sweet yet so dirty.

I shake my head in refusal.

"Suit yourself." He sighs and continues pouring the drinks before walking over to us. He hands G.M. a crystal glass before sitting in the oversized chair behind his oak desk.

He sips his drink and then clasps his hands on the desk. "So, how can I help you two lovely ladies?"

G.M. clears her throat. "As I mentioned in the lobby, Marigold has a condition similar to yours. She's been cursed since she was a baby, and I think you can help her."

I can't help but wonder what his condition is. Surely, he can touch people. He's surrounded by people daily and kissed G.M. Fairy's hand. It's clear he has no idea what it's like to be me.

He takes a deep breath. "And when you say *a condition similar to mine*, you mean..."

"If I touch someone, they turn into gold." I'm surprised by the sound of my voice.

His gaze lingers on me, and he shakes his head slightly. "She speaks."

"Marigold is a shy girl. As you can imagine, she's lived her entire life in solitude," says G.M. Fairy.

Winston doesn't take his eyes off mine. His expression is sober and intense. "I don't mind shy."

G.M. laughs. "Really? You and everyone you surround yourself with are anything but shy."

Winston shrugs and takes a sip of his drink. "So, why do you think *I* can help?"

Great. This guy is as useless as the rest of them. My shoulders deflate.

"Well, since you've lived most of your life with a similar condition, I figured you could help me get her to a place to retrieve a potion that can cure her."

I turn my attention to G.M. She never mentioned traveling to another place. All she said before we left LA was that Winston could help me. The journey here has already been enough for this lifetime. I don't know if I want to travel more, especially with a strange man who makes me uncomfortable.

Winston laughs. It's bold and crisp and, for some reason, makes my insides feel like mush. "A cure? You and I both know there are no cures to curses. Only those damn witches who brought this suffering upon us can cure their creations."

"That has been the case until now. There's a powerful wizard named Draven in New York that's rumored to have a cure for curses."

Winston gets up from his seat and faces the bookshelf behind him. "Not to be cocky, but I'm a powerful wizard. You've said before I come second to you. What makes you think this bloke can find a cure if you and I never could?"

"He's not just a wizard. He's also a vampire."

Winston looks over his shoulder at G.M. "A vampire wizard?"

G.M. flies up from her seat and leans over Winston's desk. "Yes, and apparently, he's concocted a potion to cure any curse. The secret ingredient? Virgin blood, specifically the blood of the cursed. You know how vampires have a way with blood."

Winston searches G.M.'s face before breaking out in a laugh. "You're joking."

She pushes herself back from the desk. "I'm afraid not. Apparently, if the cursed have retained their virginity, Draven can extract their blood, modify it, mix it in with a potion, and poof, their curse is gone. That means our beauty over here is as good as gold. All she needs is someone to help her get there."

My face heats, and I clench my fists. Although it's no secret that I have never known a man's touch—or anyone's for that matter—I don't appreciate two people discussing my virginity as if I wasn't in the room.

Winston looks over at me, and his cheeks flush. "Why do you need me to take her? Why can't you?"

G.M. flies back toward her seat, her back facing Winston as she speaks. "Draven and I aren't on good terms. I can't vouch for his character, but he's Marigold's only option." She turns toward Winston and gives him a knowing look. "Besides, I figured why not get two curses broken instead of one?"

Winston's eyes shift nervously.

Does that mean what I think it means? How can the owner of a sex club be a virgin? But G.M. did say his curse was similar to mine, so he must be unable to touch people in some capacity.

Winston picks up his glass and takes a long sip before walking to a large window facing a wash of darkened trees. "I have to ask. Why is this endeavor of interest to you?" He walks towards G.M. "Don't get me wrong, you've shown nothing but kindness to my friends and me over the years, but you're a businesswoman. I know there's nothing you don't do that doesn't line your pockets."

G.M. puts her hand over her heart. "Winston, you must not know me at all."

"Come on now." He smirks.

She smiles back at him

I must admit, his charm is something to marvel at.

"I am a businesswoman, but I'm a fairy godmother first, and I just so happen to be Marigold's godmother. I've been watching over her since she was a little girl. And now that she's nineteen and all on her own, my time has come to help her dreams come true."

My heart warms. Since I was a little girl, I'd always known that G.M. was my fairy godmother. She'd visit me in my room and listen to my stories and dreams. Growing up, she was my only friend, but she never allowed herself to get too close. Even as a child, I'd always felt a wall between us.

It wasn't until my father's death that she took me away from my home. The prison I'd known for nineteen years.

G.M. takes in a breath. "Besides Winston, you owe me a favor. Don't you remember that you, Beck, and Liona needed me to get you that Charming Potion last year?"

"I seem to remember that helping you open the club in this magical community was me returning the favor."

She pats his arm. "No, no, no. Allowing you to open a franchise brand of Happily Ever Endings and become wildly successful was not my favor. This is." She flies toward the office doors, opens them, and turns to face us before exiting. "Well, I have a club to explore, and you two might as well get to know each other. I'm going back to LA tonight. You have a long journey ahead of you." She winks and shuts the doors.

And then we were alone.

Chapter Three

WINSTON

I stare at the closed door G.M. just exited from, my mind racing. What the hell am I going to do now? I can't deny the magnetic pull I feel toward this girl, but this will only lead to danger. Now, apparently, I'm responsible for her, and we are very much alone.

Marigold clears her throat, and her chair squeaks as she adjusts herself. She must be as uncomfortable as I am in this situation.

Except I'm in agony because it's taking everything in me not to rush over to her and pull her against me. Obviously, that would be very bad for both of us, but the thought makes me even more anxious. It's like I'm an animal denying my natural instincts, and she's a fragile little deer, utterly unaware of my thoughts. I just hope the animalistic side of me remains hidden.

Not only does my mind whirl with thoughts of this magical woman that's consuming me from the inside out, but there's also the new hope that I could have my curse broken, making it hard to focus. Honestly, I don't believe this wizard can cure us. I've spent my whole life searching for a cure for my curse and have always come up with nothing. This vampire wizard thinks he can erase curses with a little blood and virginity? It sounds like a crock of shit. I don't want to say this out loud, though. If I can offer Marigold even a sliver of hope, even if it's just for a moment, I'll do it. Besides, G.M.'s right, I owe her.

I turn my head to face Marigold and clear my throat. "So, Marigold, it looks like you and I will spend a lot of time together." I walk over to the desk and perch myself on the edge in front of her.

She looks nervously at her hands. G.M. said she lived a secluded life, but did she live in a bunker? She's barely said two words since she arrived, and she looks frightened I'll gobble her up. Sure, that's exactly what I'm thinking, but I'm a gentleman, nonetheless.

I look at my watch. "Well, the club doesn't close for another four hours, but I can probably pull myself away in about two. I still need to chat with G.M. about the details of where we'll be heading to New York. Then we can head back to my place."

"Your place?" Her eyes are wide saucers.

Shit. I don't know why I would assume she'd be okay staying with me. We'd just met, and it seemed as if she hadn't met many people in her lifetime. Staying with me makes the most sense. Besides, I want her to be as close to me as possible for as long as she can. "Oh... um... There is an inn nearby, but I figured it would be easier if you stayed at my place."

Her eyes shift, and she fidgets with her hands.

I kneel in front of her. "Marigold, hey."

She brings her gaze to mine.

"I know you're nervous, and a lot is happening, but you can trust me. Do you think G.M. would leave you with me if I weren't someone you could trust? I promise I won't hurt you. Besides, I should be more scared of you. You could kill me with just a touch." I chuckle, hoping she will lighten up with some humor.

She turns her head away from me and furrows her brows.

I guess that didn't work. God, she even looks beautiful when she's angry. What could I have said to anger her, though?

I stand up and dust off my black slacks. "Well, do you want to stay here until we can leave, or do you want to come with me into the club?"

I expect her to cross her arms and remain seated. She's as timid as a mouse. There's no way she's stepping back into the club when it's in full swing, but I thought I would at least give her the option. Maybe she's curious. She hasn't seen much in her lifetime.

To my surprise, she uncrosses her arms and looks up at me, her eyes sparkling. "Is it safe?"

"Yes. No one in the club is allowed to touch anyone without their permission. If they do, we'll revoke their membership immediately, and we've never had to do that. Besides, you can stay with me the whole time if you want to."

Her eyes dart back and forth as if picturing the various horrible scenarios she might find herself in.

"Marigold."

Her eyes snap to mine.

I hold her stare for a moment, relishing that all her attention is on me. "If you don't like what you see out there or you feel uncomfortable, you can always come back to my office. I promise."

She breathes out. "Okay." She stands up. The space between us tightens, and I can feel her breath on my skin. Her eyes lock with mine, and we stand silent for a moment.

The only sound is the low thumping from the club outside my office doors. We're in a trance, a second in the swirling universe that's all our own. I wonder if she can feel this magnetic pull between us. I look down at her silk gloves. Do they really protect others from her touch? I'm tempted to test them out, even if it could mean my death.

As if she notices my stare and my dangerous thoughts, she wraps her arms around herself and clears her throat. "Should we go?"

I clear my throat and gain my composure. "Yes, let's go." I walk toward the door, but Marigold speaks before I reach the doorknob.

"Why are you being so nice to me?"

"Why wouldn't I be?" I turn towards her.

She rubs at her arm, not looking me in the eye. "I don't know. I just met you, and now you're offering to take me across the country and open your home to me. Why?"

I want to tell her the truth—that I've never met anyone who's had the effect on me that she has. That she is perfection personified, and every cell in my body screams to be near her. But of course, that's crazy; even saying it to myself is crazy. So instead, I say, "I owe G.M. a favor. I don't know if what she says about this wizard vampire is true, but I'm willing to travel to help you but also to help myself."

She nods. "Okay, I'm not sure if I trust you completely. I have a hard time trusting anyone, but I think I have enough to get us to New York." She walks toward me.

I shrug and lead us out the door. "That's good enough for me." Even though it's not. I want all of her trust. I want all of her. But for now, this will do.

CHAPTER FOUR

MARIGOLD

I 've only ever visited G.M.'s Happily Ever Endings in the light of day, but I imagine it looks a lot like this one with the lights low and crowded with people. Well, I shouldn't say people. Although some creatures look like humans, everyone has a mythical element, as if they're straight from the storybooks. Except I don't remember any fairytales being anything like this.

Most people wear tight leather outfits or practically nothing. Everyone is all over each other, kissing and touching. I can't help but stare, mystified by the sight that sends tingles down my body—even if another part of me feels dirty and wrong thinking about these things. There are women with scales, men with trunk-like bodies, goblins, fairies, and everything in between.

I want to stop and gawk at the people around me. Although technically, I'm also magical, normal-looking people have always surrounded me. Well, I guess not surrounded—just my father, a few of his business partners, my tutor, and doctors. If it weren't for G.M. Fairy, I wouldn't know that there were more magical beings besides me and my curse.

My steps are slow as I walk through the winding halls, but when I notice Winston is a few paces away, I speed up. I'm curious, but not enough to be left alone in a place like this. Even though I just met Winston, I trust he'll keep me safe. Maybe it's my naivety, or perhaps it's something else.

He leads me to the main room, the one we met in. He motions for me to sit at the bar and walks around to speak with the bartender.

"Can I get you anything, Hun?" says another bartender as she wipes the bar before me.

I try to find the words to respond, but I'm distracted by her antlers and doe-like features. She's a woman alright—beautiful with long eyelashes and honey-colored hair—but she seems to be a cross between human and deer.

"Are you okay?" she asks, breaking me out of my trance.

"Yes, sorry. This is my first time here." I push a strand of hair behind my ear and lean over the counter so she can hear me better. "In fact, this is my first time anywhere with this many people."

Her laugh is deep and comforting, making me feel as though she understood. "No wonder you look so nervous." She snaps her fingers. "I've got just the drink for you." She pulls out two clear bottles, pouring them into a silver canister. Her arms seem to move a hundred miles a minute as she picks up different ingredients and puts them in the container. She puts a lid on and shakes it beside her head.

"Are you making a magic potion?" I ask, embarrassed by my words the second they leave my lips.

She throws her head back and laughs. "Yes, I guess you could say something like that." She pulls out a clear glass with a high stem and pours the contents into it. The liquid is a light pink color and steams from the top. "Bottoms up," she says as she puts her hands on her hips.

I look between her and the drink. "Are you sure it's safe?"

She chuckles and wipes her brow. "You are something else. I promise this is the perfect drink for you."

Although I'm terrified of consuming this mystical drink, she went through all the trouble to make it and isn't taking her eyes off me. Before I have more time to talk myself out of it, I grab the drink and throw my head back, gulping its contents as fast as possible. When I pick my head back up, I notice the burning in my throat and chest. I cough and hold my stomach. That was the worst thing I'd ever tasted, but I didn't want to be rude, so I tried to hold back my disgust.

"Woah there, little lady. That wasn't a shot. You didn't need to throw it back like that," says the bartender. She leans in closer with wide eyes.

"What was that?" I get out between coughs.

"Alcohol, hunny. That and a little elixir that will help you relax a bit." She's still staring at me with concern.

A wave rushes through me. The room seems to blur, and all the harsh edges are gone. The colors seem brighter, and everything's lighter. I giggle. "I think I like this," I say as I swivel my head around and take in the surroundings I'm suddenly much more fond of.

"Alright, I'm good here we can…" Winston pops up next to the bartender, a clipboard in his hand. "Oh, no. What did you give her?" He freezes and watches me intently.

I don't know why he looks so concerned. I feel like a million bucks.

"She said she was nervous, so I made her a drink with the Inhibition Elixir to help her take the edge off. I didn't know she would chug it in one gulp or react so quickly."

"Ah, shit. I don't think she's ever drank before. Marigold, how do you feel?" He's pressed up against the bar, examining me.

"I feel great! I don't know why everyone's being so dramatic." I wave my hand to slap his arm, but he pulls his arm away before I can touch him.

He gives me a grave look. "Marigold," he says in a warning tone.

I raise my hands overhead, swaying my body with the music. "Calm down! I won't hurt you if you don't touch my naked skin. I'm wearing gloves, see!" I wiggle my fingers in front of his face. I liked saying the word naked. It sends a tingle down my body, and I wonder what other things I can say that will make me feel this way.

His cheeks redden, and he shakes his head.

I can't tell if he's angry or blushing.

He leans in to whisper to me–his gaze is dark and intense. "Marigold, I think you should return to my office and wait until I'm done. You're not yourself."

Although I love hearing my name on his lips, I'm offended that he's telling me what to do. I get up from my seat. "You just met me. You don't know what myself is!" I turn around toward the club and scan for something that excites me. I've never felt this confident and free in my entire life. I'm not wasting it sitting in some stuffy office.

Someone grabs my gloved arm, and my heart stops. I spin around to Winston, his gaze intense as he stares down at me. I search his body, looking for evidence that he's turning. I just proclaimed that it was safe for him to touch me as long as it wasn't my bear skin, but no one has tested this theory for a long time. Maybe forever.

His touch burns, but all I want to do is lean into it more, to feel it all over my body. I can't believe he risked everything to touch me. I'm unsure if he has a death wish or is just that confident with his life. Either way, I can't complain that he tried it. If anyone had to be the first to touch me, I'm oddly glad it's him.

Finally, he seems knocked out of a trance and parts his lips. His voice is low and gruff. "Fine, if you want to wander around in this state, I'll allow it, but I'm following you. I'm not letting you do something you might regret tomorrow when you're not in your right state of mind."

I don't know how I feel about him watching me explore a magical sex club. I can't deny the buzzing throughout my body that begs me to partake in something deliciously naughty. "Don't you have work to do?"

"Most of my work is just showing face and ensuring everything runs smoothly. I can do that while following you around."

I pull my arm away, but as I do, I immediately regret it. I miss the feeling that I'd never known. "Fine, but keep your distance. I want to have fun."

He shakes his head. "God, how much did she give you of that elixir? I might have to fire her."

I'm well aware that how I'm feeling and behaving is out of character, but I don't care. I turn and walk toward an entrance to a hallway.

The hallway is dimmer than the main lobby of the club, but the noises seem to heighten. I stop at the first door to my left. It's a black door with red trim left ajar, red light spilling from the crack.

I turn to Winston, who, just as I suspect, is only a few paces behind me. "Can I go in?"

Winston looks at his watch. "The show's about to start in a few minutes. Are you sure you want to witness it?"

I don't know what he's talking about, but I don't like his condescending tone. "Yes, I'm sure." I push open the door and enter.

Even in my confident state, the sight before me makes me nervous. It's too intimate. I want to run out, but I just made a big deal about entering. If I turned around now, I wouldn't recover from the embarrassment.

The room is smaller than the main lobby but grander than I would have guessed. It's a theater with red lounge chairs facing a stage hidden by red curtains. The lights are low and red, making everything look spooky. Heads turn to me as I enter—a hungry look in their eyes that

I'm not sure I like. People have packed the room, and only a few spots remain at the front.

Great.

I turn toward Winston behind me. He has a kind and knowing look on his face as if to say, "It's okay. I know this is too much. We can turn around."

I don't know if it's the elixir, the alcohol, or just being sick of everyone treating me like a porcelain object my whole life—I want to smack the look right off his face.

I take a big breath, my body still buzzing from my drink, and walk toward the front, sitting in one of the smaller red chairs in front of the stage.

Winston sits next to me.

"You don't have to be here with me, you know," I bark angrily.

"Do you know what kind of show this is?"

"Yes!" I lie. I'm not sure why. It's an obvious lie. Why on Earth would I know what kind of show this is?

He breathes in and props his ankle on his knee. "People are about to fuck each other on this stage, you realize that?"

That statement sobers me up a bit. How can he say something like that so casually while looking the pinnacle of class and success?

He studies my face and grabs my gloved hand.

The sensation shoots throughout my body; even with the inhibition elixir, it's all too much. My nerves ignite, and my body vibrates with anticipation.

"Let's leave while we can." He lightly rubs my wrist with his thumb as if he's touched me a thousand times before.

It's too much for me, and I pull away.

"No, I want to stay." I turn my attention back to the stage, honestly shocked by the words that just left my mouth. I most certainly do not want to stay, but I don't want to let Winston know this. Besides, a slight buzz begs me to remain planted in my seat and witness what transpires.

He sighs and drops his head into his hands.

The lights dim even lower, the heavy music increases in volume, and the curtains slowly rise from the floor.

My breath catches in my throat as I take in the sight before me. A woman sits on a large red velvet throne, naked and bound. She's gagged with a black ball, but I can tell from her sparkling eyes that she's more than pleased with the position she's found herself in.

The lights are so low that I don't notice the hulking figure hiding in the shadows behind the throne. That's until I hear his footsteps as he steps into the light and circles around the woman in the chair.

Oh, my god. It's not a man at all. I know we're at a magical sex club, but this guy is fucking terrifying.

I turn to Winston, not even trying to hide the fear and shock in my eyes. "What is that?" I mouth.

"An ogre," he mouths before grabbing my hand again, almost like he's trying to comfort me.

I want to pull back. I'm not used to being touched, let alone by a stranger that makes my insides feel like mush. But honestly, it helps. I'm feeling a little less frightened and a little more excited about what's coming.

Unfortunately, Winston lets go of me and returns his hand to his lap.

The shirtless ogre is all green muscles. Even under the red lights, his coloring is startling. He's terrifying, but the bound woman looks eager to see him. He circles her, trailing his giant fingers up and down her oiled body.

The woman is beautiful, with dark brown hair and blue eyes that shine through the darkness. I scan her body to find any evidence of her mysticism but can't find a trace.

I lean closer to Winston. Even though I'm not in my right state of mind, I still have enough wherewithal not to let my lips graze his ears. "Is she a human?" I whisper.

Winston leans to my ear; his hot breath makes my skin tingle. "Yes. That's Liona and her husband, Beck. They're the co-owners of the club and my good friends."

Luckily, the loud music covers our whispers.

I nod and return my attention to the show. G.M. was right when she said Winston's friends were anything but shy. Although I've never had friends before, I can't imagine watching my friends fuck each other in front of a crowd. This is weird.

I wonder if he gets off on this. I look over to his lap, and sure enough, I can make out the impression of his impressive length pressing against his black form-fitting slacks. I scan his body and nearly jump out of my seat when I realize his heated eyes are on me. His stare is dirtier than the performance happening before me.

I look back to the stage, my cheeks heated and my body a tingly mess. I must have missed a few parts in the performance because now the ogre is on his knees, pushing the woman's—I guess Liona's—legs even farther apart than her bounds are holding them. His enormous tongue licks up and down at a slow tempo.

Liona squirms against her bonds as if she's being tortured, but the look on her face reveals pure ecstasy. Even though she's gagged and the music's blaring, I can hear her moans from the back of her throat. Then I notice that it's not just her moans I hear—they're coming from all around me.

I swivel my head around, immediately regretting my decision as I watch people with their hands between their legs, gyrating up and down on a partner's lap, or receiving their own oral sex. Typically, this sight would absolutely repulse me. I've barely thought about sex, let alone watching other people enjoy it, but right now, my body hums with delicious need. I don't know if it's the drink or the environment in general, but I feel fidgeting and in dire need of release. I rub my legs together and fidget with the fabric of my dress. I've never touched myself that way before, but now it feels like my body knows exactly what it wants.

An urge takes over, and before I have time to think about it, I grab Winston's hand resting on his armrest. He rubs my wrist in slow and soft circles with his thumb as if this action is the most natural thing in the world. All the attention of my body goes to that spot. All I can think about is him touching me that way in other places, however impossible that would be. My heart beats wildly as I bring my attention back to his gaze, still resting on me.

It's becoming all too much. My head spins as I watch Winston's heated expression. My breath quickens, and I feel myself on the brink of something powerful. The noises vibrate my body, and my vision clouds when I feel like I can't take it anymore. I rest my head against my seat as everything starts to go dark. The last thing I hear is Winston saying my name.

Chapter Five

WINSTON

Getting Marigold back to my house was no easy feat. She blacked out in her chair, and although technically conscious, she wasn't in control of herself. She would have never made it if I weren't a wizard who could use my powers to float her back to my house. This experience made me realize how complicated her life must have been without anyone being able to touch her.

Luckily, G.M. was in the room with us during Liona and Beck's sideshow performance. Before I floated Marigold back to my place, she filled me in on the details of our journey to Draven's. I plan to leave in the morning. Technically, there's no rush, but I am more than eager to get there if there's a chance to break our curses.

I can't believe my bartender made her such a potent drink. I feel like a dick for being unable to protect her in my own club. Sure, I stayed by her side for the short time that she was in control of herself, but I know she would never have wanted to explore the club the way she did if it wasn't for that elixir. I hope she doesn't regret her decisions in the morning.

I hated myself for the way I felt watching her. I shouldn't have enjoyed seeing her lose control when it wasn't her choice. Although

I remained a gentleman and didn't take my cock out and stroke it in front of her, my thoughts were anything but gentlemanly.

I'm still hard as a rock as I use my wand to place her in my bed. She mumbles softly to herself as I magically pull the covers over her form. The moment the blanket wraps around her, she nuzzles against it, a content moan escaping her. It takes everything in me not to take myself in my hand, watching her drift off to sleep in my bed.

This is the first time I've ever had a woman in my bed. I never thought this would be possible for me, even though it technically still isn't.

Her body stills and her breath moves steadily, letting me know she's drifted off.

I know it's wrong, but I can't help myself. I crawl into bed next to her, watching her fragile features and her eyes move behind her lids.

I don't know why I'm so enamored by this woman. Yes, she's devastatingly beautiful—as if she was crafted by gold—but this feeling I have is more than that. It could be that she suffers from a similar affliction to me and that my whole life, I've been dying to relate to someone on this level, but it feels more. Like maybe we were destined to find each other.

I've never been a romantic. I keep myself too busy to even think about the love I've always lacked, but I'm finding myself becoming an entirely different person in the few hours since I met Marigold. She has softened my heart and turned it into gold.

I'm so lost by her soft breath and watching the rise and fall of her chest that I don't catch myself dozing off next to her.

CHAPTER SIX

MARIGOLD

My eyes shoot open, and my chest rises and falls as if I just outran a beast. It takes me a second to adjust to the darkness—the only light comes from the full moon outside a large window to my left.

I don't recognize my surroundings. I'm in a stranger's bed, and the feel of the sheets makes my body react strangely. I pick up the covers to find myself naked and damp with sweat. How did I lose my clothes, and how did I end up here?

As if an answer to my silent thoughts, I hear floorboards creak. I shoot my attention to the edge of the bed.

It's him.

He's walking closer to me, wearing nothing but a pair of tight boxer briefs. His disheveled, curly brown hair frames his face, and his blue eyes shine through the darkness as they devour me.

My heart beats wildly, anticipating his thoughts by the expression on his darkened face.

I find my voice lodged at the back of my throat. "What are you doing?" I get out between heavy breaths. There's already a wetness between my legs.

"Watching you," he says in a low voice as he kneels on the edge of the bed before leaning forward on all fours.

"Why are you watching me?"

"I like to watch. Always have." He crawls closer to me.

From the look in his eyes, it seems like that's not all he wants to do to me. Consume me from the inside out? That sounds about right.

He crawls toward me until he's holding himself over my body—his breath on my neck. We're only inches apart.

I catch his eyes with mine, searching for his intentions. I can't find anything to indicate he's backing down. "What are you doing?"

"What does it look like I'm doing?" He brings his lips to my neck. The tiniest movement and his skin would be on mine.

"It looks like you're trying to get yourself killed." I've never felt such a longing. I want nothing more than him to crash into me. To ruin me. But my life has been full of wants, and it doesn't seem like my happily ever ending is happening anytime soon.

My whole body hangs in anticipation of his response. I finally feel the air escape from his parted lips. "If I'm not buried deep inside of you in the next five minutes, I'll die anyway, so fuck it." He crashes into me, his hard body rolling onto me as he captures my lips with his.

I grab the back of his head, running my fingers through his velvet hair. I rub against his length, aching for a release I've never known.

He kisses down my neck, allowing me to catch my breath when I realize what's happening. We're touching. We're kissing. And he's not turning into gold. Tears well in my eyes at the realization until suddenly, it's not just his cock that stiffens. Starting from his legs, his body becomes solid on top of me. I open my eyes and look down, catching his once wispy hair, now strands of gold.

I killed him.

The pressure of his body crushes me. I sob as I try to push him off of me, realizing I'm trapped.

I scream, tears falling down my cheek.

***

My eyes shoot open, and I'm covered in sweat. My limbs tangle in a mess of white silk sheets, and I bolt upright, taking in my surroundings. I'm in a room similar to the one in my dream.

That's right. It was only a dream. None of that happened.

I'm in a room lit by the rising sun, bookshelves taking up the walls parallel to me, stacks of books in every corner, dark furniture and fabrics, and a musky smell like sandalwood.

My brain floods with the events before I blacked out.

Oh no. I can't believe I acted that way; Inhibition Elixir or not, I'm mortified. Then I remember the person responsible for all my new experiences and the dream slash nightmare I just woke up from. My head swivels around, trying to find him, but it doesn't take long to realize he's sleeping beside me.

I jump once I spot him, nearly falling out of the bed. He's practically lying in the middle of the bed. Either one of us could have rolled onto each other in our sleep. Maybe this guy does have as much of a death wish as he did in my dream.

Heat floods my core at the thoughts of the steamy embrace I just woke up from. I'm quickly chilled once I remember how it ended—exactly how it would in real life.

I watch him momentarily, lying on his side with his hands underneath his head. He looks so peaceful in his slumber, and I wish I could watch him like this forever. I wish I could trace the elegant swoop of his nose or the cupid's bow of his full lip. I shake my head. I don't know what G.M. was thinking. Winston has to be the most dangerous option to take me to New York. With the thoughts running around my head, I'll kill him before we make it on the road.

What's another death? A small voice nags at the back of my thoughts, chilling me to the bone. Sadness washes over me like a summer downpour. I shake my head. I can't keep sitting here alone with my thoughts. They're too dangerous.

"Um, Winston," I try softly, still unsure of myself.

He stirs slightly but doesn't wake.

"Winston," I say, a little louder this time.

He finally rolls over to his back, lifting his tanned arms above his head. His veins flex as he rotates his wrists, and I don't know why this sight affects me. I imagine watching his veins flex on his forearms as he holds himself over me, pumping in and out of me.

Shit. What's wrong with me? Could this still be the effect of the elixir? I thought it would have left my system after passing out in the club, but magical potions may have dangerous, long-lasting side effects.

His eyes slowly blink open and widen once he takes me in. He reaches for the bedside table beside him and grabs a pair of circular tortoise-shell glasses. Once he places them on the bridge of his nose, he jumps out of bed. "Marigold, I'm so sorry. I just laid down for a moment, and I guess I dozed off." He fidgets with the sleeves of his black shirt from yesterday.

If I thought he was handsome the night before, the way he looks right now brings a whole new meaning to the word. The glasses, messy hair, and disheveled clothes from the night before are all too much for me.

I clear my throat. "You know, you could have killed yourself falling asleep next to me." My voice betrays the butterflies in my stomach.

He chuckles and runs his hand through his hair. "I'm not afraid of you, Marigold."

It feels like he tries to say my name as much as possible, and I can't say I dislike thinking of me on his lips.

"Well, you should be. I'm dangerous."

"I don't know if you realize this, but I'm also cursed. I know what it's like to be dangerous." His eyes lose a bit of their sparkle.

That's right. I keep forgetting he's cursed. His life seems so full. He owns a club. He has friends. He seems experienced in all aspects of life. I crave to know more about his condition. It only seems fair since he knows almost everything about mine, but it's rude to pry. If anyone knows what it's like not to want people to ask you about the most painful part of your life, it's me.

I rub my arm and look down, realizing I'm also wearing the same clothes from last night. I don't know how I'll get my belongings before our journey. G.M. said she was leaving last night, and now we're hundreds of miles away from my home.

As if reading my thoughts, Winston speaks up. "You have a bag in the corner. I assume that it has extra clothing. I didn't want to snoop."

"How did it get here?" I think for a second. "Actually, how did *I* get here?" There's no way he could have carried me.

"Magic," he says matter-of-factly.

A chill runs down my spine, thinking about him using magic to get me from one place to another. I wonder what else he can do to my body with his magic. I shake the thought out of my head.

Winston gives me a devilish smirk before walking to his dresser. It's like he can read me like a book. "Why don't you go wash up and change?" He motions to the bathroom connected to his room. "We need to pop into town before we get on the road. There are a few things I need to pick up."

We're going into town? I've never walked through a town before, let alone a magical community. The thought both terrifies and excites me, much like this whole situation does.

I get up from the bed and walk toward my worn duffle bag in the corner. "So, you're really going to take me to New York?"

"Really, really!" He replies in a sing-song voice.

I sigh as I drop my bag on the edge of the bed and search through its contents. Wow, it does contain everything I need. Magic is pretty cool. "I still don't know how I feel about this. We don't even know each other."

He turns to me and rests against his dresser, a pair of socks in his hand. "I think we know each other a little better after last night."

His words send a fire to my stomach. "If anything, last night is a testament to how weird this whole situation is. You let me get drugged! I shouldn't be going with you."

He puts down his sock and pleads with his hands. "Woah! Wait a second. I apologize that you unknowingly took something you didn't want to at my club, but that wasn't my fault. And you'll be happy to know that I fired the bartender. My club should be a safe place."

"Wait, I don't want her to get fired." I liked the deer woman even if she did slip me something I wasn't aware of.

"It's already done."

Yikes. I guess I don't want to get on his bad side.

I grab my clothes for the day and attempt to enter his bathroom. Before I get through the doorway, Winston grabs my gloved arm. "Listen, I'm going to keep you safe. Nothing bad will happen to you while you're with me." His gaze is intense, and between that and the heat from his touch, I'm one second away from melting into the floorboards.

I nod and walk into the bathroom, his words ringing through me. Although it's nice that he's trying to comfort me, I'm not worried about my safety. I'm worried about everyone else's.

***

Winston's cottage sits not too far from the bustling town center. After changing out of my clothes from the night before, the two of us make our way to the cobbled streets with tall stone buildings on either side. Colorful flower boxes line all the windows, and white doors swing open and closed as people bustle in and out.

"Only about three thousand creatures live in the magical community, so it's pretty quiet around the shops even though it's one of the only places we gather," Winston says as we walk side by side. The early morning sun reflects off his mop of hair, making it look lighter than usual.

A warm breeze blows through the streets, and the scents of fresh baked goods hit my nose. My long cream skirt twirls around me.

"This isn't busy?" I ask in shock, tucking my blue-gloved arms into myself. I've never been around so many people, and even though the nearest creature, a bunny as tall as Winston, is a hundred feet away, it still feels too close. All around me are creatures with tails, wings, fins, and antlers. Gnome children play in the street or run out together from the candy store. Everything sings with life and laughter. I love it, but it's a lot all at once. I need about a week to sit on a bench and adjust to all the sights and sounds.

Winston searches my face before cracking a smile. "Oh boy, will you be shocked in New York."

I don't like the sound of that, but before I have time to question him about what to expect in New York, Winston calls to a couple ahead of us. "Beck, Liona!"

The ogre and human turn towards us, a small bundle in the woman's arms.

Oh god. It's the couple from last night. Unfortunately for me, I remember everything. My cheeks heat at the thought of having to have a civilized conversation with them. How can they perform so publicly the night before and then walk down the streets the following day like nothing happened? I would be mortified.

"Winston!" Liona smiles as she looks me up and down before leaning in to hug Winston.

All I can think about is what this woman looks like naked. I practically saw inside of her.

The ogre nods at Winston but doesn't hold the same joy as Liona. He remains stoic and terrifying as he was last night.

Winston leans over the woman's arms and smiles at her bundle. "How's little Felicia doing?" he asks in a baby voice.

So, the bundle must be a baby. I can't help my curious thoughts at what a half-ogre, half-human would look like, but the baby is so bundled that all I can see is a peek of dark hair.

"Great! That Gilda is a miracle worker. She put her down last night, and this little one slept a full eight hours, thank God! Lord knows I needed my rest after last night." She looks up at her hulking ogre, her eyes sparkling.

The ogre looks down at her and smiles. It's the first smile I've seen from him, and by the way he looks at Liona, I can tell he's in love.

Although I don't know these two, it warms my heart to see such a terrifying monster turn into a big ol' softy around the woman he loves.

Liona looks back at me. "I saw you last night. I'm Liona." She juggles the baby into one arm and then extends her free hand to me.

My cheeks heat, thinking about where exactly Liona saw me—sitting in the front row while an ogre licked her pussy until she exploded into multiple orgasms.

"Oh, hi," I get out meekly, staring at her hand but not attempting to touch it. Although Winston proved he could touch my gloved hand without consequences, I'm nervous about testing it on someone new.

Winston places his hand on the small of my back, and my nerves ignite. "This is Marigold."

Liona smiles at Beck with a knowing look before looking back at me. "Well, hello, Marigold. It's so good to see Winston with someone. Are you a wizard as well?"

"Uh." My words get lost on my tongue, and I look toward Winston for help.

"No, she's not a wizard, nor with me. Technically, we are with each other right now, but G.M. is cashing in on that favor we owe her. She wants me to take Marigold here to New York."

Liona and Beck's faces grow serious.

"Do you need our help?" Beck questions, his voice low and loud as I would have guessed.

"No, don't worry about it. I just have to drive her to New York to meet another wizard there. Honestly, I'm surprised the return of her favor is so simple."

Liona's chest deflates. "Okay. Well, let us know if you need anything."

The baby in her arms fusses. She unravels the swaddle, propping the baby on her shoulder and patting her back. She walks in place while twirling, and I can finally witness the baby's face.

With big brown eyes, a thick head of brown hair, and skin so light green you barely notice, it has to be one of the cutest babies I've ever seen.

Felicia smiles at me and waves. Something about babies makes everything seem better.

"We should probably get this one home," Beck says, putting his arm around his wife. "You two have a safe trip."

"We will!" Winston says. I don't notice until he applies pressure, but his hand still rests on my back. He leads me to the other side of the street, waving to Beck and Liona as we walk. We head into the shop with a general store sign over its door.

A warm seed of happiness plants itself in my chest that Winston didn't disclose all the details of our journey to his friends. I should thank him for not telling them, but words are always hard for me. Especially with him,

He had a right to tell his friends the real reason for our journey. If G.M. trusted Beck and Liona to open the club with Winston, they must be trustworthy. But I like that Winston understands the sensitivity of my condition and that I might want to own a sense of normalcy.

We both know what it's like to live a life shadowed by our curse. I didn't realize how nice it would be to have a co-conspirator. I've missed this connectedness even though I just now realize it could exist. Maybe having him as my travel companion won't be a horrible idea after all.

CHAPTER SEVEN

WINSTON

"What are you doing?" Marigold asks as I pull into the small shop.

I turn the car off and pull down my sunglasses to look at her. The midday sun reflects off her golden hair, and her beauty consumes me. But she just asked me a question, which I haven't answered. I'm just staring at her like I lost my last brain cell.

I clear my throat. "I want to stop and get a snack, and I thought you'd like to see the sunflower garden." We've only been driving to New York for a few hours, but I'm eager to stretch my legs and show Marigold something she's never seen.

"Sunflower garden?" Her sparkling eyes betray her skeptical expression.

"Yeah, come on. You'll love it." Before she has time to protest, I exit the car and jog over to her side to open the door. I extend my hand.

She tries her best to turn down the smile forming at the corner of her lips, but I catch a glimpse of it as she puts her gloved hand in mine.

The bell from the shop rings overhead as we walk into the desolate gift shop. Marigold swivels her head around to take in all the various candies, snacks, sunflower-themed decor, and Florida props.

I grab a bag of sunflower seeds and toss them on the counter before the woman reading from a magazine. "Do you want anything?" I ask Marigold as I look through my wallet for my credit card.

"Umm..." She twirls around, tapping her protruding lip, until she spots something and brings it to the counter.

I examine the container filled with pink and blue fluff. "Cotton Candy?" I ask, smiling.

She shrugs. "I've never had it before."

I nod and place it on the counter.

After the cashier rang us up, I led Marigold out of the shop and to the back of the building.

"Wow," she exclaims as she walks towards the tall yellow flowers, reaching up to touch their petals.

"I take it you've never seen sunflowers before?" I walk next to her, watching her bemused expression.

She shakes her head. "I never really left my father's estate growing up. And although he had an impressive garden, we never had sunflowers." She steps away from me and follows the clearing with the sunflowers looming overhead.

I watch her for a moment. Every few paces, she reaches up on her tiptoes to examine the face of the flower. Each time looks like the first.

It's been a while since I've witnessed such a gentle beauty. Everything is new to Marigold, and although she does succumb to her fear, she also has a side eager to take everything in. I want to be the one to show everything to her.

I knew from the moment I laid my eyes on her that she would be the person to ruin me, but every second with her digs the knife deeper into my soul.

"Are you coming?" She calls from ahead. I smile and run after her.

Chapter Eight

WINSTON

I've always considered myself an excellent driver, but driving with Marigold hinders my skills. Her eyes are framed with elegant black sunglasses, and the wind swirls around her, making her addicting scent travel toward me. I can't stop staring at her. Of course, her safety is paramount to me, but her beauty seems as dangerous as her touch. We've been driving for the last five hours, but her beauty is still an anomaly I can't help but gaze at.

The car swerves as the road bends, and I snap my attention back to the road.

"Are you okay?" Marigold asks, and I can feel the heat of her gaze on me.

"Yes, sorry. I just got distracted for a second."

I pat the side of my 1964 Ford Falcon Sprint as a plea for this pile of metal to help get us to New York safely.

"Have you been to New York City before?" Her soft question surprises me since she's been silent most of the car ride.

I pull my sunglasses down the bridge of my nose and look at her with a nod. "Yes, a few times."

"Have you traveled to many places?" she asks, tucking a strand of hair behind her ear.

I subconsciously slow the car down to hear her better through the wind rushing overhead. Convertibles have their perks, but right now, I wish I had a less noisy car to hear every sharp syllable of Marigold's words.

"Yes. I've been to most of the fifty states and several countries as well. What about you?" I immediately regret asking it. What a stupid question. Of course, she hasn't been anywhere.

"No," she says solemnly. "My father wouldn't let me go anywhere because of my condition."

"Where's your father now?"

Her voice saddens me even more, and I turn to see tears well in the corner of her eyes. "He's dead."

"I'm so sorry." I wish I could comfort her. I wish I could take all the pain away.

It's silent for a moment. My personal question seemed to ruin any chance of us getting to know each other better.

Marigold clears her throat, and my heart skips a beat. "What's your curse?" Her cheeks are bright red, as if it took all her courage to ask me this question.

I want to answer her boldly and honestly. It's only fair. I already know so much about her curse. But mine is different and more personal. I don't know if she can handle it. "Mine is complicated."

"Well, you seem to live a normal life. How complicated could it be?" Her boldness surprises me.

"It may seem like that, but my life is anything but normal."

She leans against the headrest. "Well, the whole magical sex club isn't that normal, but whatever your curse is seems to be the complete opposite of mine."

"I told you, Marigold. We're more alike than you think." I wink at her, and she blushes.

I love that I can turn her colors. My cock stiffens, thinking about how I could make her react in different ways if given the chance.

I haven't had a chance to take myself in my hand since meeting Marigold. I'm not shy about pleasuring myself, even in public. It's the only way I can relieve my urges. Hell, that's what Happily Ever Endings is all about, but the thought of Marigold seeing me touch myself makes me uneasy. I'm not sure she would like the sight, and I'd never do anything to make her uncomfortable. I wonder if she's touched herself before. The thought washes over me until it's all I can think about. My car swerves slightly off the road, making the tire skid into the rocky gravel. Marigold yelps, and I straighten up, but once back on the paved road, the car sinks to one side with an awful sound. I drive the car back onto the side of the road.

"Fuck!" I yell before stopping the car and exiting to see the busted tire on the passenger side. Why am I not able to fix this tire with my magic? What good is being a wizard if you can't avoid simple problems?

Marigold peers over the side. "That doesn't look good."

"No, it doesn't." I kick the tire and run my hands through my hair. I don't even have a spare.

"What do we do now?" She asks.

I take my phone out of my pocket. Of course, there's no service. "We need to walk up the road to see if we can find a phone or Wi-Fi so we can get it towed to a shop."

Marigold's eyes bulge. "But it's almost dark."

"I know, so we better hurry." I open the door for Marigold to exit. She steps out of the car like a deer, learning to walk.

I feel like a jackass. The only reason I'm tasked with taking Marigold to New York is to protect her, but I can't stop thinking about fucking her long enough to get us there safely.

"I'm sorry, Marigold."

She holds onto herself, looking like she's about to crumble. "It's okay, it's not your fault."

Except it is. Me and my tortured thoughts.

***

"God, I would kill for a burger right now," I say as I stare at the dark road before us. It's been an hour of walking, and we still haven't seen any sign of civilization, and now my phone is completely dead.

"And a milkshake," Marigold says, rubbing her stomach.

I'm glad to see that her mood has lightened. Maybe she's just delirious from her exhaustion. "What's your favorite food?" I ask.

"Umm." She taps her gloved finger to her face. "Probably a grilled cheese."

I chuckle. "Okay."

"What?" she scolds, but I can hear the smile on her lips. "Grilled cheese is good!"

"You're right. It is. I just wouldn't say it's my favorite food."

"Okay, Mister Cultured. What's your favorite food?"

"Probably sushi."

She nods, the moonlight illuminating her soft features. "Well, I haven't had sushi before."

"What? You've never had sushi? That settles it. We're getting sushi. It will be the first thing we do in New York." It's still so shocking how sheltered Marigold has been her whole life. She's only five years younger than me, but her innocence makes her seem much more youthful. But at the same time, she seems older. She's dealt with some heavy shit throughout her life, which can make someone grow up fast.

"Okay, deal." She sighs. "We just have to get there first."

Although I'm loving the lighthearted conversations that have transpired between us on our trek to rescue, I'm still disappointed in myself for getting distracted and jeopardizing our safety. I want to confess my idiotic ways, but I also don't want to admit to Marigold that we traveled off the road because I was thinking about her touching herself.

When I'm about to give up hope, a building appears in the distance.

"Look!" Marigold exclaims excitedly as if it's Disney World instead of a shitty motel in the middle of nowhere. She picks up the hem of her skirt and runs toward the motel. I follow behind.

When we get to the front desk, the single tooth man informs us there won't be any tow trucks out this late.

I look at the watch on my wrist. It's already nine at night. We'll need to stay the night and worry about the tire in the morning.

I rub at my temples, feeling the day's stress roll over me. "Alright, could you give us a room?" I fish my wallet out of my pocket. "Two beds, please."

"I only have a room with one queen," the man says.

"What? There were barely any cars in the parking lot. How can you only have rooms with one bed?"

The man shrugs and offers no rebuttal.

"Fine, just give me two rooms."

Marigold touches my arm. "I don't know if I want to stay in a room by myself." Her voice is frail, and her cheeks red.

I study her face, surprised that she'd be willing to share a room with me with one bed. I look around the motel lobby. Wallpaper crumbles off the walls. Flies hang on a sticky trapper, and cigarette smells block our airways. Her fear of this place must be overtaking her fear of me.

My blood pumps violently in my veins thinking about sharing a room with Marigold. This is only going to make this journey more painful, though. Nothing can happen between us, and taking care of my urges in a room alone with her will be impossible. I'll do whatever it takes to make her comfortable, even if that means subjecting myself to torture.

I slam my card on the desk. "Fine. One room, please."

Chapter Nine

MARIGOLD

I'm utterly surprised at myself for the energy I have flowing through my veins. My body should be begging to crawl into a ball and sleep for the next twelve hours after the hike we just took to get to this shitty motel. My heart pounds in my chest, and my only thought is that Winston and I are about to share a bed... together.

Technically, we've already slept in the same bed. I just didn't know he was there. I shouldn't have told him I didn't want my own room. I could kill him—but the thought of his body being so close to mine excites me too much. Him thinking I'm just scared to sleep alone is a good enough cover for my heated thoughts. I don't know what's wrong with me. It's like my brain has been taken from me and replaced with a horny pornstar, but all I can think about is Winston.

Of course, he's devastatingly handsome and charming, but there's something more. The fact that we're both cursed makes us feel like we're just parts of a whole. I doubt he feels the same. I'm just some dumb girl he has to carry along to pay his dues.

"I can make a pallet on the floor, and you can take the bed." His words knock me out of my trance as he grabs a pillow and the quilt folded on the end of the bed.

"No, you don't have to do that." I'm surprised and embarrassed by how eager my words sound.

He stops, his eyes burning holes into me. "Are you sure that's a good idea? You seemed to think otherwise last night."

I shrug and walk toward the sink at the far end of the room, trying to hide the blush on my cheeks. "You're probably exhausted from driving all day. Besides, you didn't die last night. I'll separate us with pillows." What's come over me? It's like I'm this new brave woman I've only ever dreamed of becoming.

"Okay, if you insist." He rustles with the covers.

I stare at my reflection in the mirror. My hair is messy from the wind, and my skin is blotchy and dull. I splash water on myself and take a big breath before returning to the room's bedroom area.

I've only ever seen motels in movies, but it looks exactly as I would expect. The carpet and linens are red and old, and various stains line the ceiling and walls. Meth was definitely dealt here. Normally, I would be grossed out and frightened, but I only want to climb into bed with Winston right now. I don't know why. It's not like we can do anything, but simply being near him excites me.

The lamp on the bedside table illuminates Winston's frame under the covers. His shirt and jeans rest folded on the chair next to the bed, which means he's only wearing his underwear.

I should be creeped out that he would take off most of his clothes and jump in bed with me, but for some odd reason, it doesn't. I want him to wear less. In fact, I want to wear less, but I know that would be far too dangerous.

We left our luggage in the back of Winston's locked car, so there's nothing I can change into. I gingerly pick up the corner of the musty quilt and slide into the bed with Winston.

My heart beats wildly as I stare at a stain in the shape of an elephant on the ceiling. I listen to Winston's shallow breaths as he flips to his side.

It's silent. So silent that it's loud.

"Goodnight," I say.

"Goodnight," he replies after a beat, switching off the light next to him.

I flip to my side, facing the pillow between us. Everything in me begs me to pull the pillow away to look at him sleeping. Maybe just watching him will calm the strange heat growing between my legs.

To my surprise, the pillow slides down the bed, first revealing Winston's mop of hair and then his crystal blue eyes, still bright even in the darkness.

He jumps a little when he catches my eyes with his. "Oh, sorry. I uh... I just wanted to see if you were asleep yet."

I can't stop the grin that forms at the corner of my lips. "Sure, you were."

He pulls the pillow to his chest, wrapping his muscular arms around it. "You don't believe me?" He grins. "Well, what else would I be doing?"

"You wanted to watch me sleep," I whisper. Although the motel is desolate, it feels like we need to be quiet. Like we're two misbehaving children on a sleepover—whatever the heck that's like.

"Marigold, I've already seen you sleep. Why would I want to watch you snore and catch flies with your open mouth?"

I chuckle. "Hey!" I slap his arm. Once my gloved hand meets his skin, I freeze. It's like I forget I'm not supposed to touch anyone until I feel him. Obviously, I can touch him while clothed, but each time seems like a risk. I wonder what else I can touch on him with my gloved hands.

I rub his muscular forearm with my thumb, staring at the spot I'm touching. The air around me thickens, and suddenly, all playfulness is gone, and in its wake is only weight.

I look up to Winston's eyes, and he's staring at my lips.

I find my voice. "Can I test something?"

He nods. The moonlight from outside our window illuminates his chiseled features.

I take the pillow from his arms, throw it behind us, and trail my fingers up his arm. "Are you scared?" I whisper as I slide my fingers over his collarbone.

"I told you. I'm not scared of you, Marigold." His expression tells a different story. His eyes watch me intensely, and his breath seems stuck at the back of his throat.

"Tell me when to stop." I scoot closer to him, still not letting our bodies touch as I trace his jaw and lips.

I jump a little when he grabs my other gloved hand and rests it against his cheek. He puckers his lips and kisses each of my gloved fingers.

I gasp. No one's ever kissed me before. It's such a simple gesture, and it's only my fingers, but it sends a rush of heat down my body, and I feel myself dampen.

I move my hand down his body, pushing away the covers. He's muscular and lean and looks like a model in a magazine. My fingers trace his hard pectorals and the ridges of his abdomen. He sucks in a breath through his teeth, and I pull away. I scan over him, looking for any signs of him turning.

"It's okay," he says as if in pain. "It just feels good. Too good."

"It does?" My cheeks heat.

He nods.

Power surges through my veins. I've always known my touch was powerful. It could turn the strongest men into a pile of metal, but I never thought I could also wield a touch that brought a sound like the one Winston had just made.

I bring my hands back to him, lightly tracing his muscles again.

"I wish you could feel this," he whispers.

"Maybe after this trip," I whisper back, subconsciously leaning closer to him.

He takes in a big gulp as my hands trail lower to the waistband of his underwear. I stick in my finger, and a low growl comes from the back of his throat.

I look up at him, and he shakes his head. "That's where I'm going to have to stop you."

My heart drops, and I pull back. "Okay," I say, trying to hide the disappointment in my voice.

"Believe me, I don't want you to stop, but that's where my curse starts."

"What do you mean?"

He sighs and rubs his face. "I guess now is as good a time as any to tell you."

I scoot closer, resting my head on my hands and staring deep into his eyes. I want to know his secrets. I want to know everything about this mysterious and magical man.

"My curse is that I can never be intimate with someone, or the person dies."

My heart pounds. From an outside perspective, his curse doesn't seem worse than mine. At least he can hold someone's hand, hug someone, bump into people on the streets—all the things I would have killed to do my whole life. But I can understand how he wouldn't see it this way. It's a painful and embarrassing blow. I guess that explains why he's still a virgin.

"I'm sorry," I whisper.

He gives a sad smile. "It's okay. I can't complain compared to your curse."

My thoughts race. "But why do you own a sex club? Isn't it torture to watch people like that and not be able to do anything about it?"

"Oh, I can do something about it." He gives a low laugh.

I scrunch my face. "What do you mean?"

He chuckles and leans closer to me, his breath on my ear. "Haven't you ever heard of touching yourself?"

Goosebumps spread across my skin. "So, you watch people have sex and pleasure yourself?"

He shrugs and pulls back. "It's the only thing I can do."

"So that doesn't count as being intimate with someone?" I gulp. The words are heavy in my throat. "Touching yourself in front of someone?"

"My curse is like yours. We're good as long as no one touches me, and I don't touch them. *A touch for pleasure, will reap pain. A mortal who indulges you, will be slain.* You know how those witches love to have a catchy saying to their curse."

I do know. My father repeated my curse over and over throughout my life, to make sure I remembered the danger I possessed.

I want to hear more about the witch who cursed him. I wonder if he was old enough to meet her or if his curse was generational like mine. But diving into his history isn't my greatest concern right now. My nerves twitch restlessly. I need more from him, and I can't stop the want seeping from my pores. "So, you could touch yourself right now, and I could watch?" I don't even believe the words came out of my own mouth. My heartbeat is in my head, and I want to crawl into a hole and die. Both my body and mind have betrayed me.

Winston stares at me with his lips parted, searching my heated expression. "Would you want me to do that?"

No! The good little girl inside me screams. You just met this man! You have another day of travel and a curse to break with him. It would be completely awkward if you watched him touch himself to completion, but the bold new woman inside me shuts her up. "Yes," she says, her voice layered in confidence.

Winston closes his eyes and breathes out. "Okay, but you have to touch yourself too."

"What?"

A devilish smirk appears on his face. "It's only fair."

"But I don't know how."

He scrunches his face as he studies me. "You don't know how to touch yourself?"

I'm sure my cheeks are beat red, shining through the darkness. "No."

He bites his lip and scoots closer. In a whisper, he says, "I can teach you. Would you like that?"

I close my eyes and try to focus on my breathing. His question makes me feel dizzy. "Yes," I answer breathlessly. But even in my roused state, I still have some sense. "But you can't touch me."

He holds himself up and stares down at me. It's like a switch flipped, and the charming gentleman I knew before disappears. His gaze makes me feel like I'm already wearing nothing— like he will devour every inch of me. He leans down to my ear. "I don't need to touch you to make you scream my name."

My breath heavies. His words send a new rush of wetness to my core. I don't know what he means, but it makes me all sorts of hot and bothered.

He gets out of bed and rummages through his pile of folded clothes, pulling out a wand before crawling back in bed. "Do you trust me?"

"Yes." Even though I shouldn't, I don't know him well enough, I do.

He lies next to me and flicks his wand once. I feel the clothes disappear from my body under the blankets.

I look underneath the quilt. "Where did they go?" My cheeks heat at the sight of my nakedness.

He motions with his eyes behind me.

I turn and look to see my clothes neatly folded on the chair next to me. My heart pounds, and I pull the blankets close to my naked skin.

"Relax," he soothes, scooting as close as possible to me without touching me. He must sense my nervousness, but how could I not be? Besides allowing myself to be intimate for the first time in my life, there's also the risk of his death. Just one wrong move, and his bare skin could be on mine. This position is the most dangerous I've ever been in. It's terrifying and exciting all at the same time. "This might tickle at first." He flicks his wand, and I feel light pressure against my nipples.

A gasp escapes from me at the sensation. All my nerves melt away, and all I want is more. I pull the blankets down my chest, revealing my bare breasts as the invisible sensation continues.

He sucks in a sharp breath and closes his eyes. "God, you're beautiful," he gets out between breaths. He blows out a breath of air, regaining himself, and leans over to whisper in my ear. "I wish I could taste you." He keeps his wand pointed at my breasts.

The image comes to my mind—his full lips around my nipples, his tongue flicking back and forth. The sensation is almost enough to bring me somewhere. It feels as if I'm about to jump off a cliff.

"Are you wet yet?" He whispers, his breath tickling my ear.

"What do you mean?" I barely get out.

"Feel between your legs."

I do as he says, trying to concentrate on getting my hand to my cunt and not the insatiable, magical movement continuing on my nipples. My fingers slip into me. "Yes," I pant.

"Move your hand. Let me show you how you can touch yourself."

I do as I'm told.

Winston moves the wand down my body. The sensation at my nipples ceases, and he flicks his wand at my cunt.

"Winston," I cry out, shocked by the sensation. It feels like his fingers are dipping inside me and then using my moisture to run up and down my lips.

"Stroke up and down like this." He stops at the top and circles a small bud I didn't even know existed. "This will bring you to your orgasm."

"What does that feel like?" I ask between gasps. I feel on the brink of something powerful and overwhelming. I don't know if I can take any more.

"My sweet, Marigold. I can't wait to be the first to bring you to your edge." He leans down to my neck, his breaths heavy as he uses his magic to circle my bud.

My body feels weightless but heavy at the same time. I've never felt anything so good, and I buck my hips at the magical pressure. I grab my breasts and flick my fingers over my nipples.

"Good girl. Just like I taught you," he smiles down at me, his eyes watching my fingers work over my pointed nipples.

I've become a greedy little thing, wanting more. I want Winston pressed against my body. I want his lips on my neck. I want him inside of me, but I know that can never be.

But maybe after this trip, a hopeful voice rings through me. If this is just a small example of what life could be life with the ability to touch, I'm more than eager to get to New York and break this curse.

"I'm going to make you come, Marigold," he whispers, and as soon as he says it, my body convulses.

"Winston," I moan as stars blind my vision. God, this feels heavenly. How have I missed out on this my whole life?

Winston doesn't let up the pressure until my body slacks, and I'm panting for him to stop. He leans to my ear and whispers again, "Good girl, now you can do it to yourself."

I don't believe him, though. I don't think I could replicate how he made me feel.

"I want to watch you now." Although a wave of relief from the tension I'd been feeling all day—actually, the past two days since I met Winston—has lessened, I want more. A new soft buzz already ringing through my body.

"Anything for you." His eyes are dark and seem to burrow into the deepest part of me. His gaze takes my already depleted breath.

Chapter Ten

WINSTON

It's taking everything in me to control myself. Watching her come undone under my magic was like experiencing bliss for the first time. And now she's begging me to take myself in my hand while she watches. I think I'm in love with this girl, but that could be my dick talking.

I lean over and place my wand on the bedside table before lying on my side, supporting my head with my hand.

I bring my attention back to Marigold, noticing she's removed the blankets from her body. I take in all of her. From her angelic face, down her perky and full breasts, to her cunt covered by golden curls.

"Fuck." I throw my head back and bite my lips. The sight of her overwhelms me. "I won't last long, Marigold."

She smiles at my words, and her cheeks redden. I bet she's wet again, and I long to stroke my fingers through her velvet skin.

"That's okay," she whispers, lazily trailing her fingers over her nipples. Goosebumps pepper her skin. Just moments before, she was a fragile flower. Now, she's a brazen woman, ready to take her pleasure in her own hands.

I slowly roll my boxers down, watching as her eyes follow my movements.

Her breath hitches, and her eyes widen in surprise as I grab my length and pull myself from my boxers.

"Is it supposed to be that big?" She doesn't take her eyes off my cock.

A laugh barrels through me, and she snaps her attention back to my face as if she's worried she said something wrong. "You sure know how to boost a man's ego, Marigold." I rub my palm at my tip, lathering it in my precum, dripping from me.

One of her hands grazes lazily down her body. "But wouldn't that hurt a woman?"

"Maybe at first," I answer honestly. "But I promise, from what I've seen, the women seem to enjoy themselves." I slide my hand down my shaft, imagining Marigold's tight pussy gripping me.

Marigold gains the courage to bring her fingers to her core. "I'm already wet again." She moans.

I shut my eyes, trying to control myself for a moment longer. "Marigold, you're going to ruin me." I slow my strokes and open my eyes to watch her continue exploring her body. One hand plunges deep into her cunt, fucking herself with her fingers. Her other hand circles her nipples. Her breath quickens, and her eyes remain focused on my cock.

"I wish I could touch you." She pants.

"Oh god, Marigold. If I could touch you right now, I'd fuck the words right out of you."

My words seem to excite her, and her fingers move up to her clit. She spreads her legs for me so I can watch each delicate movement.

"After this trip. We'll be cured, and you can be inside of me."

I stay silent. I don't want to ruin this moment together, but even in this state of delirious pleasure, a pang of doubt rests in my mind.

I scoot closer to her, so my breath is against her lips. "Be in this moment, right now, with me. Come for me, baby."

She continues to stroke her pussy, fingers slipping through her wetness.

"That's a good girl, fuck yourself, just like I taught you." I can tell my words affect her because it seems like that's all it takes before she sputters toward her edge.

Her body tenses and she throws her head back, arching her back in turn. "Winston!" she cries.

The sight of her pleasure sends me right after her. I milk myself for every last drop on the sheet between us. All I want to do is let my come rain all over her perfect tits, but I don't know how she'd feel about that. I continue stroking until there's nothing left in me, watching Marigold as she comes down from her orgasm.

As she blinks her golden doe eyes, her expression sobers.

I wish I could wrap my arms around her and whisper sweet nothings in her ears, but I can only watch her. She's sure our curses can be broken, but I'm having difficulty believing that. I want to tell her that if this is all we can have, it would be enough for me. But I know she doesn't want to hear that. "How do you feel?"

She lies on her back and stares up at the ceiling. She's silent for a moment before she gulps. "New."

Chapter Eleven

MARIGOLD

I wake to sunlight streaming in from the blinds. It takes a second to remember where I am, but the stench of old cigarettes quickly reminds me. The scratchy quilt against my skin proves I'm still naked, and I turn to see my folded clothes still resting on the chair next to me. The memory of the events of last night floods every inch of me, and I want to remain swimming in them—soaking in the feelings that passed through me.

Today is day three since meeting Winston. It only took three days for my life to change completely. I'm a new woman now. One that's tasted pleasure so sweet I don't think I can live without it. I know it's impossible to fall in love in three days, well, except in fairytales. But what else could Winston and my story be? I'm a woman with a magic touch, and he's a powerful wizard. Our story could be straight from a storybook.

I wonder if last night was as important to Winston. There's still so much I don't know about him. He owns a magical sex club. He probably engages in that kind of activity all the time. To me, it feels special, but for him, it could just be another weekly occurrence.

I subconsciously put a metal layer around my heart. I can't let myself get too attached too quickly.

A weight presses down on my arm, covered by a blanket. I look down to see Winston's arm.

"Winston!" I yell, jumping out of bed.

He startles, sits up, and rubs his eyes. "What's wrong?" He reaches for his glasses on the bedside table. This is my favorite version of him—disheveled and groggy. He's so sexy that I almost forget the anxiety running through my veins. Almost.

"You had your arm on me. You could have touched my skin." The soberness of the moment makes me embarrassed by my naked body. I quickly jump into my skirt and pull my shirt over my head.

He leans forward and pats the bed. He's still wearing nothing besides his boxers.

A chill runs up my spine, remembering the impressive package he keeps hidden.

"Marigold, it's okay. Nothing happened. Come back to bed."

I stay where I am. "We need to be more careful until we get this curse broken. We can't let ourselves fall asleep next to each other like that."

He clenches his lips and nods. "You're right. We need to be more careful. When we return home, we'll figure out a sleeping arrangement that keeps us safe."

I look at him as if he's grown a second head. "What are you talking about?" My mind sputters to all corners of possibilities. One part of me celebrates that he's already decided to take me back home with him. It's not like I have anywhere else to go, but I think I'd want to go with him even if I did. Another part of me rests confused.

"Why would we need to be safe when we get back home?" I turn my attention to putting on my gloves. Maybe he just misspoke. He's lived a whole life with his curse. It must be hard for him to imagine a life without it.

"Marigold."

I look up to see him sitting on the edge of the bed, his expression serious.

"What?"

He stands and walks closer to me. "I think we need to think of the possibility that there might not be a cure to the curse."

I shake my head. "No. G.M. said that Draven could help us. Why would she lie?"

He removes the space between us and holds my gloved hands in his. "I'm not saying she's lying. I'm saying that this Draven character could be. Listen, I've spent years traveling around the world looking for a cure to my curse. I'm not saying he won't be able to break ours, but I was hoping you could accept the possibility that he could be a hoax. I've met dozens of people claiming they could help when they couldn't."

I shake my head and pull away from him. I can't believe he's already preparing for the worst. After last night, I know what I want, and I'll never be satisfied unless I have all of Winston. I can live with that. What I can't live with is the danger I will continue to be to him.

"How can you say that? What happens to us if the curse isn't broken?"

He grabs my hands again. "We'll be okay. We can be together like we were last night."

"I may not have experience, but I know last night wasn't truly together. Besides, I could have killed you. I don't want to wake up one day to a statue of you." Horrible images flash from my past. I'm dangerous. I can't hurt someone I love again.

I try to pull away from him, but his grip tightens. "Marigold, that might be all we have. Of course, I hope the curse will break, but we have to be realistic. This might be all we have."

"No!" I yell, pulling away from him. "If the curse can't be broken, we can't be together. I can't be with anyone."

"Marigold, I'm not afraid of you. I'm willing to take the risk."

Tears stream down my cheeks. "Well, I'm not." I charge toward the door, but Winston follows behind and grabs my arm. "Marigold, please don't do this. This is just the beginning."

He has to know. I whip around, the truth bubbling in my throat. "I killed my father."

Chapter Twelve

WINSTON

The pancakes sour in my stomach as I sit across from Marigold in the small-town diner.

After she stormed out of the motel room, I went to the front desk and called for a car service to replace our tire. Our journey is back in motion, but everything between Marigold and me has reached a standstill.

She hasn't said a word to me since she told me how her father died. I know I should be the one to say something first. She's obviously dealing with tremendous hurt over her father's death, but I don't know what to say.

I want to tell her it's okay and I don't look at her differently, but I think she told me that to warn me off—to show me how dangerous her touch could be. She didn't say she killed him with her touch, but I can read between the lines. That's why she doesn't want to be with me if we're unable to find a cure for our curses. But don't I get a say in it? I should be able to choose my own risk.

I push away my uneaten pancakes. I can't keep swimming around in my thoughts. "Marigold, we need to talk."

She doesn't look up from her cut-up waffles that she's moving around in her syrup.

I take this as a sign to go on, so I lean in and whisper, "I don't care that you caused your father's death."

She looks up at me with anger in her golden eyes. "Thanks. Well, I do."

Shit. That was the wrong thing to say.

"What I mean is, I am prepared to take that risk. You don't need to protect me."

She slams her fork down on the table. The sparse number of patrons turn their attention towards us. She leans in to whisper, "Do you know what it's like to live with the guilt of someone's murder? You might be okay with it, but I'm not okay with having another person's death on my hands." She's crying now. "Sure, my father was a horrible person. You know he was the cause of my curse? He was such a greedy bastard that he cheated a witch out of her money, and so she cursed his only daughter. *For your greed will be rewarded with gold—a daughter's whose touch no mere mortal can ever hold.*"

She is talking at a million miles a minute. I want to stop her, but I'm also eager to hear more about her life.

"My mother was so upset that she left us. It was just my father and me, but he didn't consider my curse bad. No, he used it to make himself extremely wealthy." Her tears are streaming now. "He made me touch people. People that no one cared about—homeless people, prostitutes. He would drug me while I was sleeping so I couldn't fight him. I didn't know it was happening until I turned eighteen, and he decided it was time to tell me the truth." She looks me dead in the eyes. "I loved my father. I did. Yes, he kept me locked up in my room and barely spent time with me, but I loved him."

"I know," I soothe, grabbing her gloved hand.

She pulls away. "But he told me as if it was my fault, like I was the one who murdered those people. He said that if I tried to leave, the police would arrest me. He held it over me. I was just so angry and scared. I wasn't thinking. I just wanted to hit him." She cries louder, and I have to wave off the waitress passing by.

My heart breaks watching her in so much pain. I want to tell her how much I relate—I know exactly what she's feeling. But this isn't about me now. She needs to get this out and have hope. Maybe the curse can be broken, however unlikely that may be. It has to be for Marigold.

I grab her gloved hand.

She tenses at first, but when I don't let go, she finally relaxes and puts her other hand over mine.

"I just can't have it happen again." She looks up at me with watery eyes.

At this moment, I would tell her anything in the world to stop her hurt. Her life is so filled with pain, I wish I could take it all away. I would die for this girl, I'm sure of it.

"Marigold, listen, I'm sorry, but your father's death wasn't your fault. He was an evil man keeping you prisoner."

She still won't look at me. "I didn't want to kill him, though, and I did."

I know there's nothing I can say to take away her pain. Even if she were cured, she'd still live with this for the rest of her life. But I'm determined to help her heal as much as she can.

"Let's just not think about this right now. For all we know, this wizard can cure us, and we don't need to worry about this."

She nods and wipes her tears. "Okay." She turns to look out the window, peering out to the road from our booth. She pulls away from my grasp. "But you're right. I need to be realistic. I can't let myself get too attached. We need to slow down and see what happens."

Her words gut me deeper than I thought possible. My body burns from the lack of contact. I want to throw a fit and demand that she continues her descent of falling in love with me. Hell, I'm already madly in love with her. How could I slow down? But I don't want to hurt her. If this wizard ends up being a crock of shit, as I suspect, I'll worry about it then. Now, I need her to be happy, even if that means she's holding back from me.

I nod. "Okay, we'll slow down. I can be slow." A small smile creeps to the corner of her mouth, and suddenly, it's all worth it. I can do this. I can love her in secret, at least for the rest of this trip.

Chapter Thirteen

MARIGOLD

We're back on the road with only a few more hours until we make it to New York City. Before us lies an open road that can lead to my happily ever after. But Winston's concerns ring through me. This could be our last trip together. I fell for him in three days, and it could be over before it even started.

I lean against the passenger door, resting my head on my arms as I stare at the scenery rushing past me. At first, the convertible annoyed me, but now I like the feeling of my hair flying freely around me. I've lived my whole life in captivity; at least my hair deserves to be freed.

Things feel different now between Winston and me. It's not as tense and difficult as before our conversation at the diner, but I can feel the uncertainty between us. Even though I'm the one who said we need to take it slow and guard ourselves until we find out if this Draven guy is legit, I don't really mean it. I don't want to take anything slow with Winston. My whole life has been slow, like watching paint dry. I want to reenact last night repeatedly until I'm sick of looking at him, which I don't think will ever happen. But I have to guard myself and him.

He's experienced a lot more life than me. If he thinks it's near impossible to break our curses. I have to consider that.

At least we can be friends. He knows me better than anyone else ever has, which is sad to think about since it's only been three days. I might as well take the time to get to know him better.

I stretch my arms wide and turn to Winston.

He smiles at me, and a warm rush floods down my body.

I lean back against the seat. "Tell me about your childhood."

He scrunches his face at me and laughs. "My childhood?"

"It's only fair. I told you about mine."

He bobs his head back and forth. "True, but isn't that a bit of a personal conversation? Aren't we supposed to be taking things slow?"

"No, this is friends talk. Friends talk about their childhoods."

He gives me a heated look, pulling down his sunglasses. "Is that what we are, friends?"

My cheeks heat. "Yes."

His eyes trail down my body, and he licks his lips. "We're not going to be friends."

I can't stop my body's reactions to his words. All of me heats, and it takes everything in me not to throw myself on his lap and take out his cock. Of course, that would mean death to us both, but even the danger thrills me. *God, what is wrong with me?*

I breathe out, trying to compose myself.

Winston smiles and turns ahead. It's obvious he knows how much his words affect me, from the smug grin on his face. I want to kiss it right off of him. God, this taking it slow thing is torture.

I breathe exasperatedly. "Well, whatever we are, I think it's only fair to know more about you."

He's silent momentarily, gripping the steering wheel and staring ahead. "What do you want to know?"

I think for a moment. "Did you have any siblings?"

"Nope, just me."

"Did you grow up in Florida?"

"Nope, Connecticut."

"What were your parents like?"

He hesitates. "My mother was wonderful."

I don't reply, eager for him to tell me more. I never knew my mother, so it's nice to hear that he had fond memories with his.

"She married my father when they were young. She was a lower wizard, so she came from a relatively poorer family."

Winston drips with class from the way he talks to the clothes he wears. It's surprising to me to hear that he grew up poor

As if he can read my confusion, he continues, "My father was a powerful wizard from a very wealthy family. My mother was beautiful. Everyone wanted her, especially my father, who got everything he wanted."

"He sounds a lot like my father," I say, already feeling the tears well.

"Yeah, they sound like they're cut from the same cloth to me."

"Is he the reason for your curse?"

He nods. "My father was a womanizer. He was good at charming women and telling

them exactly what they want to hear."

"I guess you get that from him."

He smiles at me, but it doesn't reach his eyes. Maybe that was an insensitive comment.

"I don't know about that. My soul knows you. That's why I know the words you want to hear."

His soul knows me? I feel my heartbeat throughout my body. How can he turn a normal conversation into something so romantic? God, this Draven better be the real deal. I don't think I can live without Winston and his words.

I shake my head and try to get this conversation back on track. "So, how did your parents end up together?"

"My father convinced my mother to sleep with him and created me. His family wouldn't let him impregnate a girl without marrying her. He didn't love her, just her beauty. He loved every woman's beauty." He sighs. "One day, a beautiful woman caught his attention, and they started a secret love affair. When he was sick of her, he cast her to the side, and the woman was heartbroken. The young woman ended up killing herself over it."

"Oh my God."

"Yep. Well, apparently, that woman was the daughter of a powerful witch who was, as you can imagine, extremely upset over her daughter's death. So, she cursed my father for his actions. Well, actually, she just cursed me. Because of his infidelity, any child my father had would never be able to be intimate with someone. She ended his family's bloodline."

"That doesn't seem fair. Her curse just affected you!"

He turns to look at me. "Just like your curse, Marigold. These damn witches seem to overestimate these men's love for their children. Personally, my actions causing my children to be cursed for the rest of their lives would be my greatest sorrow. But my father, he couldn't give two shits." His eyes water. "He mostly left my mother and me alone, so it wasn't too bad. My mother taught me to be a powerful wizard and a decent human. I'd only see my father a few times a year."

"Are your parents still alive?"

He shakes his head. "My mom died when I was seventeen. Cancer. It's so frustrating that I have all this power, but I can't use it for the things that matter most, like saving the ones I love."

"What about your dad?"

He shrugs. "Last I heard, he ran through all his money and died of liver failure. That was when I was twenty-one and well on my own."

"Have you been on your own since you were seventeen?" Maybe that's why he seems so mature.

He nods. "When my mother died, I was so lonely. I tried to form relationships with women, thinking that would help, but it just resulted in pain. I didn't want to tell them about my curse, but I couldn't let them die. I started my journey to find a cure to my curse; that's how I met G.M." He smiles.

"And you found nothing." I sigh and look down at my hands.

"Yes, but I learned how to live with my curse. I found the magical community. I discovered the adult clubs where I could feel connected to others, even if it was on the most basic level."

My mind flashes to Winston's club and his patrons. It's hard to imagine Winston sitting alone in the front row of those performances, pleasuring himself. For some odd reason, it doesn't make me jealous; it just makes me wish I was there with him.

"Is that enough for you, though, spending your whole life watching other people?"

He shrugs. "What other choice do I have?"

I sigh and stare ahead. It's obvious that Winston has no faith in Draven, and yet he still doesn't seem hopeless. He's perfectly content being with me without touching me. I wish I could say the same for myself, but I care about him too much to let him be a casualty for my wants.

The conversation lulls, and just when it feels like there's nothing else to say, I see it. In the distance are the bright city lights and the monstrous buildings. I lean forward on the dashboard. "Is that it?"

Winston nods and smiles. "Yep, welcome to New York City, baby."

Chapter Fourteen

WINSTON

I've always loved New York City. The buildings, the people, the mixture of life—it makes you feel part of something greater. But watching Marigold take it in for the first time brings a whole new meaning to my love for the city.

Of course, we can't walk around much. Scarves and long layers cover most of her skin, but she still feels uncomfortable taking the chance. We slowly drive down the busy streets, Marigold practically hanging out of the window as she stares up at the tall buildings.

I know the perfect sushi shop in a somewhat desolate area of town. I order Marigold a California and Philly roll because I know eating raw fish for the first time isn't a good idea.

"It's okay," she says as she hesitantly takes her second bite, seated at the small bistro table.

"Okay? Are you insane?!"

She laughs and covers her mouth. "I think it's hard to get over that it's cold. I don't really like cold food that feels like it should be served hot."

I shrug. "I think you just need to eat it a few more times. It takes getting used to. I'll feed you sushi until you love it!"

She giggles and shakes her head. "Are we going to Draven's club tonight?" she asks.

I look at my watch and then study the light gray circles under her eyes. We've been traveling all day. Marigold's been to my club, but a New York club will be an entirely different experience. She needs a good night's rest before she tackles that animal.

"No, let's get some rest tonight, and we'll deal with that tomorrow."

Her shoulders roll back a bit as if she was hoping for my answer. "Okay."

My pulse quickens, thinking about having to spend another night with Marigold. I wonder if she'll want to share a bed with me again. Probably not. She's made it abundantly clear that we need to distance ourselves until we figure out Draven. I wonder if she'll really end our relationship if her curse can't be broken. Could our first time together have been our last? The thought pains me, but I must respect her wishes. Of course, I can make it very difficult for her to resist me. Yes. That sounds much more fun.

I stand up and push in my chair. "Alright, let's go find a hotel."

***

"We'll take two rooms, please. Preferably next to each other," I say to the woman at the front desk of the boutique hotel. I can't help but catch Marigold's expression from the corner of my eye. She looks as shocked as I hoped.

"I have two rooms with a connecting door. Will that work?" the woman replies.

"Perfect." I smile as I take the two keys from her.

This hotel is a giant improvement from the shitty motel we stayed at the night before. It feels wrong that Marigold and I were intimate for the first time there instead of here, but from the sounds she made last night, I doubt she minded.

"Two rooms, huh?" Marigold says as the elevator doors close before us, and we make our way up to the seventh floor.

"Is that okay? I figured since we're trying to be *friends* and all, it would be easier if we weren't sleeping in the same room." I can't help my smirk.

"Mhm." She clenches her jaw and stares straight ahead.

I smile to myself as we walk out of the elevator and to the doors of our separate rooms. "Here you go," I say as I hand her the key. Our hands touch for a moment, and she leans into it, looking up and catching my gaze with hers.

Her lips part as if she has something to say.

We stay in our trance for a moment longer until I shake my head. "Well, I guess I better get to bed. We've got a long day ahead of us."

She nods slowly. "Right, right." She turns toward her door. "Goodnight."

"Oh, Marigold."

She turns to me with bright eyes.

"If you need anything, you can just knock on the door separating us."

She holds her breath and nods. "Right. Thanks."

When I reach my room and shut the door behind me, I can't wipe the smile off my face. I can read her like a book. I know she wants me as much as I want her.

I walk toward the dividing doors to our rooms and open mine. If she opens hers, then I'll know she can't handle this *friend* business as much as I can't.

I change and crawl into my bed with no intention of falling asleep. I'm hyper-aware of every sound, every touch my body craves.

After thirty minutes, which feels more like an eternity, I walk toward Marigold's dividing door. Maybe I'm not as strong as I thought. Maybe I read this all wrong. Marigold doesn't crave me the way I crave her. I rest my head against the door, ready to give up, and beg that she let me lie next to her. It's torture being this far away from her.

Suddenly, the door opens, and I fall forward, taking Marigold with me. We fall until we're lying on the floor, my body on top of hers. Luckily, I catch myself with my outstretched hands, and the only places we touch are clothed. My mouth rests just inches from hers.

We stare into each other's eyes, both shock and fear running through my veins. We're so close, and I feel every inch of her small frame under me. I imagine she can feel how hard I am. It takes everything in me not to capture her lips with mine. I know it would mean death, but right now, experiencing heaven would be worth it all. I'm sure of it.

Marigold breaks the trance with her words before I can take us both out—Romeo and Juliet style. "Winston, I'm sorry."

I take two long blinks before removing my body from hers. "Are you okay?" I examine her from head to toe.

She stands, dusting off her long silk nightgown. Her cheeks are bright red. "Yes, I just got scared."

I stand before her, straightening out my black sweatpants–subtly trying to adjust my massive hard-on. "Did something scare you?"

She looks down at the ground and tucks a strand of her hair behind her hair. *Fuck. Her golden hair.* I want nothing more than to have it wrapped around my hand as I pound into her from behind.

I shake my head. God, I can't keep my mind in check when I'm near her. Apparently, working at a sex club hasn't made me grow used to these feelings. There's nothing to get used to, though. All the feelings with Marigold are brand new.

"I'm just not used to sleeping in an unfamiliar place alone. Can you..." She stops herself. "Never mind, I'm just being silly. Sorry to wake you." She turns and rushes toward her bed.

"Marigold, stop." I grab her arm covered by her long silk sleeve, and she turns to face me. "Do you want me to sleep with you?"

She takes a small step toward me, her eyes on my lips. "Yes."

I'm sure she can hear my heartbeat out of my chest. She does want me as much as I want her. Well, maybe not as much. I fully believe I love her more than humanly possible. But maybe that's why it's possible for me. I'm not entirely human, and technically, neither is she. Maybe that's why this connection between us feels otherworldly.

She sucks in a deep breath and turns toward her bed, pulling down the covers and crawling in.

I follow after her to the other side, making a wall of pillows between us.

I hear her turn toward me. "Oh," she says, I assume, after seeing the barrier.

"Goodnight, Marigold."

"Goodnight," she says, a hint of disappointment in her voice.

I wish I could tell her I feel the same way. This is exactly what I'd hoped would happen. She'd beg me to sleep with her, and then we'd stare into each other's eyes as we brought ourselves to completion. Of course, it wouldn't be enough, but it would be something to satisfy the constant need I feel for her. Now I realize I need to show her how possible it is to share a bed—to lie together without risking each other's lives.

We can have a life together, whether or not our curses can be cured. Of course, in this dream life, there's never a night where I don't bring the hue to her cheeks and a moan to her lips. But for now, I want to show her just how safe I can be, even if it pains me to do so.

One thing's for sure, I'm not sleeping at all tonight, and from the constant tossing and turning from the other side of our pillow wall, neither is Marigold.

Chapter Fifteen

MARIGOLD

I didn't sleep at all last night. I'm trying to enjoy the walk through Central Park, the drive around the Empire State Building, and all the other experiences New York City has to offer, but I'm exhausted. Sleeping next to Winston didn't make falling asleep any easier.

I know I'm the one who said we needed to take it slow and try to be friends, but I'm regretting that decision. After experiencing Winston's magical touch, I wanted nothing more, even if it wasn't real.

Winston's doing an excellent job as a tour guide. The city brings him to life, and his eyes sparkle as he explains the history around each building. I can tell he's been here many times before, and it fills me with excitement to think he could take me on more trips.

I want to see the world. I've lived my whole life in such a tiny box. I don't plan to spend too long in one place once this curse is broken—and it needs to be broken. Not only do I want to travel, I want to travel with Winston.

Our connection is more than physical. Our souls are two pieces of a puzzle. Both of us spending life alone. Both of us wanting to be seen beyond our limitations. It's like I can see his thoughts behind his eyes.

He looks at me as if I'm the answer to his turmoil. To him, the curse has already been broken.

I wish I could look at him the same way. But my curse killed the person closest to me, even if he was the person that hurt me the most. I can't let that be Winston's fate. No matter what happens. I care about him too much.

Winston was right when he said New York would be a shock to me compared to the magical community. New York is a never-ending stream of people, and my anxiety about bumping into them is at an all-time high. But Winston keeps me safe. He makes me feel secure even if I'm his biggest threat.

Winston parked the car on a less crowded street. We're walking side by side through an alleyway when he stops at a set of stairs leading down. "Follow me." He smiles, and his eyes shine.

"Where are we going?" I ask.

"It's a surprise. Do you trust me?" He offers his hand.

I search his expression for a moment before placing my gloved hand in his. "Yes."

He leads me down the stairs to a small green door. He reaches into his pocket and pulls out his wand, flicking it at the brass doorknob. The door swings open, and Winston smiles at me before ducking his head inside.

It takes me a second for my eyes to adjust to the darkness. There are candles in various corners of the room and an old lamp on the counter at the front of the shop.

"What is this place?" I ask as I stare at the vibrant fabrics hanging from oak built-ins around the small space.

"Why, it's a garment shop," says a small man who appears behind a book at the counter.

"Reginald! It's great to see you!" Winston exclaims as he stomps to the man and slaps him on his small back.

"Winston! Good to see you, my dear boy. What brings you to the city?" The small man hops on the counter and strokes his black beard. He pushes his circular glasses up his nose and looks in my direction. "Ah, you've brought a lady friend. I don't think I've ever seen you with a companion."

This is the second time someone has commented on Winston's singleness. He seems to have so many friends, yet his lifelong loneliness is still apparent to everyone else. It makes me sad. It makes me want to wrap my arms around Winston and prove to everyone just how capable of love he is, but we're supposed to be playing the friend role, so I refrain.

"This is Marigold. I'm taking her to a man named Draven at his club tonight. Have you heard of him?"

Reginald gives Winston a serious look. "Yes, every magical being in New York has heard of Draven. I know those types of clubs are your thing, Winston, but I must warn you. I haven't heard the best things about that man."

My blood heavies. Draven is our only hope. I guess he doesn't have to be a good person to have a cure for our curses, but fear spikes at the back of my neck, thinking about what we might need to do to get his cure.

Winston sighs and runs his fingers through his waves. "Yes, G.M. Fairy told me as much, but she seems to think he could help myself and the lady, so we're heading there tonight."

Reginald sighs and shrugs before climbing a ladder from the desk. "Suit yourselves. I guess she needs a dress for the occasion, then?"

"Yes," Winston says, smiling at me.

"A dress? But I have dresses." Although it's nice that Winston would take me to a magical shop to find a new outfit for tonight, I don't feel comfortable wearing clothing that might not protect people from me.

Winston steps closer to me, staring down into my eyes. "Yes, but you need a special dress for the occasion. This might be the night our curses are broken."

"Winston," I say between gritted teeth. Although my heart warms that he has more hope about Draven, I can't help the anxiety of being forced to wear clothes I'm uncomfortable in.

Reginald clears his throat as he skims through the clothing at the far end of the shop. "I know the shop looks a little run-down, but I promise you I'm the best garment maker in town."

I whip around, suddenly feeling like the rudest thing in the world. "No, I'm sorry, it's not that. I bet your dresses are lovely. It's just that..."

"She has a curse. She needs a dress that protects others from her skin."

I glare at Winston. I thought we had an unspoken rule about not disclosing information about our curses to new people.

"It's okay, Marigold. This is Reginald's specialty. He's used to dealing with people with curses. These garments are magical. Think of anything you want a dress to do, and he can make it happen."

I scrunch my brow. "What can a dress do to help my curse?"

He smiles as if he's been waiting for this question. "I've been thinking of a dress that covers you from your neck to ankles but offers the illusion of showing more. A dress that can change to look however you want but always covers your skin. Could you do that, Reginald?" He calls up to the shop owner.

"Of course! Transformative dresses are my specialty."

I think for a second. "So basically, the dress would be transparent in some places to show my skin? How would I make it change?"

Reginald calls from somewhere high above us. "I'll explain it when you have it on. Anything else you want from this dress?" Reginald says as he walks from behind us, a notepad in his hand.

I startle, not expecting him to come from there when his voice was high above us seconds ago.

"Um." I think for a moment. I've never had a custom dress made, let alone a magical one. I wrack my brain for some suggestions of my own. "Can it be sparkly?" I finally ask.

Reginald smiles at me, and I realize it's the first time I've seen his tiny white teeth. It makes me feel good to have made him smile. "Of course, my dear." He opens a small closet door and shuts it behind him.

I exchange a glance with Winston as loud rustling and banging comes from the door. I never thought making a magical dress could be so noisy.

After a few minutes, the door swings open, and Reginald emerges with a bundle of white, shimmering fabric. It trails behind him as he walks toward us.

"There's a changing room behind you." He offers the fabric to me, and I lean down to grab it. "Oh, and here are some translucent gloves to go with it."

I grab the two white gloves that definitely don't look invisible. I give him a skeptical look.

"They'll change to translucent whenever you will them. You need to put them on one time for them to sync to your mind, and you can change them to look however you like, whenever you like."

I stare down at the fabric in my hands. They feel thick and expensive, not to mention the magical elements I can't even believe they hold. "How did you make these so fast?"

He laughs. "Good one." He walks toward a ladder behind me next to a changing divider.

"When did that get there?"

Winston leans down to whisper in my ear. "Magic."

"Ah." I nod. I don't know if I'll ever get used to all of this, but I hope my life will continue to be this full of wonder.

I step behind the wooden divider and into the shimmering dress, pulling the straps over my shoulders. It fits me like a glove. I feel the weight of it from the top of my neck to my ankles, but when I look down, I see a form-fitting dress with ample cleavage and a high slit. I roll the gloves over my hands and watch in awe as they change from white to translucent, giving the illusion that nothing is covering my arms.

I step out from behind the divider, eager to see myself in a mirror.

"Step over here, darling. Let me see you," Reginald says from the top of his ladder.

I do as he says, and he adjusts something at my shoulder. I'm nervous about him touching me, but he seems experienced with curses and confident in his dress. I guess this test is as good as any to see if the dress works.

"Alright, all good. You can step over there to look at yourself in the mirror."

I turn, and Winston catches my gaze. Maybe I don't need to look in a mirror. It's like I can see the reflection of myself in Winston's eyes. Well, at least, how I would hope to look. I doubt the true image of me would ever be as impressive as the way Winston sees me.

"You look beautiful." He pulls at his collar as if the room just got much warmer.

Suddenly, I feel hot and bothered as well.

He shakes his head slightly and then motions to the mirror next to him. "Take a look."

I slowly walk to the mirror and gasp once I see myself. Of course, I've seen myself naked before, but this feels like seeing myself for the first time. My body has always been a weapon, one I try my best to hide. Now everything is on display in the best way.

The magical dress hangs by two small straps on my shoulders. The neckline drops low, revealing much of my breasts that I didn't even know looked this voluptuous. Sparkles line every inch of the dress like the fabric was made from the stars. I finally noticed that the dress wasn't white anymore. Colors swirl all around it. One second, it's yellow, but when I look closer, I realize it's pink.

I turn back to Reginald. "Why is it changing colors?"

He hops off his later and bounces toward me. "It's a mood-changing dress. That's the only sparkly fabric I had, but I'd figured it would be a nice touch."

"What do the colors mean?" I ask, looking down as the dress swirls as if it has a mind of its own.

"Some colors vary from person to person, and you'll figure it out as you wear it more often, but blue means scared, yellow means happy, red means mad, and aroused means pink."

My cheeks heat, realizing the reason it's a mixture of yellow and pink is that I'm both happy and a little aroused. Now Winston and Reginald know it, too. I don't know if I like this mood-changing feature, but it's too late to tell him to make a new one.

"Let me show you how you can change the dress," Reginald says as he holds up the end of my dress. "Now I want you to think about what you would look like if you were covered from your neck to your ankles."

I close my eyes and focus on an image of myself in my mind. I open my eyes again and gasp. In the mirror is a reflection of myself in a long dress with sleeves and white silk gloves covering my hands. "How did it do that?"

"Magic," Winston and Reginald say in unison.

I shake my head. I don't know why I ask anymore.

I immediately miss the image of myself in my new dress, seeing my assets on display. I close my eyes again and imagine what I looked like before. Once I open my eyes, I'm back to wearing the beautiful sparkling dress. I've always been powerful and hated it, but loving how I look in my own skin, this is the kind of power I could get used to.

I tuck a strand of my golden blonde hair behind my ear, looking at how the sparkles compliment the golden hazel of my eyes and the small number of freckles on my nose. "I love it." I beam, not looking away from my image.

Winston steps from behind me, placing his hands on my shoulders. The reflection shows his bare hands on my seemingly bare shoulders, which sends a pang of anxiety down my body. But it's not my bare shoulders, I tell myself.

"I've never seen you so beautiful."

His contact makes my dress flood pink. "I know."

"But it's not because of the dress."

I turn to give him a scrunched-face look.

"Because of the way you look at yourself in that dress. Your face lights up."

I nod and look back at my reflection. "I guess it does."

Winston lowers his lips to my ears. "As much as I'd love for you to keep the dress on. It might cause quite a scene if you step out in the daylight like this."

He straightens and walks toward the counter. "Reginald, box up the dress and find me a pair of gloves. Marigold and I have a hot date we must prepare for."

CHAPTER SIXTEEN

MARIGOLD

I jump at the knock at my door, making me smudge mascara near my eyebrow. "Fuck." I mutter as I grab a tissue to wipe it off.

Someone knocks again.

"One minute!" I yell.

I know it's Winston. I mean, who else could it be? Why couldn't he just have used the connecting door that's already open?

I stomp toward the front door, my heels clicking against the tile. When I swing the door open, I have to catch my breath. Winston is always a sight to behold, but seeing him in a black fitted suit with his hair gelled back, making his jawline look more cut than usual, numbs my body.

He reveals a bouquet of red roses from behind his back. "These are for you." He smiles.

"Oh, thank you." I grab them, still gawking at him.

"You look beautiful," he says as he examines the full length of me.

"Thank you. You look nice as well." I can feel my cheeks heat. God, we haven't even got to the club, and all I want to do is pull him into the room and rip his clothes off.

He wiggles his fingers in front of me.

"Are those the gloves you bought at Reginald's?" I ask.

"Yes." He leans in and cups my face. "So now I can touch you."

Of course, that's why he bought the gloves. I don't know why it hadn't dawned on me sooner.

My skin pricks at his touch. I don't think anyone has ever touched my face before.

He lines my lips with his fingers, staring at them. "Damn, I hope this Draven guy is the real deal," he says, as if he meant to just say it to himself.

I sigh. "Me too."

Winston steps back. "Well, we better get going. Our ride awaits."

***

Winston jogs in front of me as we step out of the hotel. He rushes toward a limo parked on the curb and opens the door.

"We're taking that to the club?" I can't hide my excitement. I've always wanted to ride in a limo. I'd only ever seen them in movies, and I never thought I'd have the chance to be in one.

"Yep." He grins, and it takes everything in me not to kiss it right off his face.

It's odd. I've never even gotten close to kissing someone, but somehow, I think I'd know what to do, especially with Winston. It's like my body knows him.

I run to the door like a giddy schoolgirl and flash Winston a smile before ducking into the limo.

Winston scoots in next to me. "Sparkling wine?" he asks as he picks up the twin glasses and chilled bottle in an ice bucket.

I scrunch my lips with a smile. "I don't know. Is it drugged?" My dress sparkles bright yellow, letting him know this is a joke.

"I'd never need to drug you, Marigold. Your body reacts to me stone-cold sober." He focuses on pouring the bubbly liquid into the glasses.

My dress changes to bright pink, and I'm thankful his attention isn't on me.

When he turns to hand me my glass, his eyes wander down my body, and he licks his lips.

I'm surprised when he leans in, his lips inches away from my ear, and whispers. "I know we're trying to take it slow, but maybe we can speed things up tonight? I don't think I can take it a second longer." His breath heavies as if he can barely contain himself.

The heat between my legs is the only thing on my mind, and although caution races in the dark corners, my want overtakes all reason. "Yes," I get out breathlessly.

Winston presses a button on the door, and the black divider slides down slightly. "Driver, we're ready to go." He presses another button, and the divider slides back up.

"It's relatively sound-proof, so he won't hear your screams." In one swoop, he wraps his arm around my waist and pulls me onto his lap, my ass against his hard length.

The swift movement catches me off guard, and for a moment, I'm sure our skin must have touched. "Winston!" I yell, stiffening in his grasp.

"Shhh," he soothes. "Relax, your skin and my hands are protected." He grabs my thighs in both hands and stretches them apart. He grinds against me. "God, I can't take another second without touching you. You look too damn good." He bunches my dress up with one hand, and his silky gloved finger drags against my inner thigh with the other.

I suck in a sharp breath. "Winston," I moan urgently. The sensation of his touch on me is almost too much. Before, his magic had felt like his touch, but this is more. He's actually touching me, even if a barrier protects him.

"Fuck," he moans as he jerks his dick against my ass. His fingers rise higher and higher up my thigh until they're just inches from my entrance. "I want you to be a good girl and soak these gloves all the way through."

I throw my head back with a moan, still careful not to let my face touch his neck. I'm trying to suppress the noises rising from my throat. Winston said this space was relatively soundproof, but he will make me scream.

He lightly trails his finger along my entrance, and I shudder. His touch is so deliciously soft it's almost too much. I wish it was his skin touching me and not the silky fabric of his gloves, but it feels so good right now I barely notice. I buck my hips.

"Stay still," he whispers into my ear as he dips a finger inside of me. "Ah, fuck, you're so wet my glove is soaked already. That's my good girl." He strokes his finger up and down, spreading me wide. His strokes increase until he gets to my clit.

"Winston, it's too much," I yell.

"Oh, no, baby. It's not enough. It will never be enough. Not until I'm so deep inside of you that you're dizzy."

The thought of Winston's hard length thrusting in and out of me visualizes before me. Winston fucks me with his finger and inserts two more.

I moan from the extra girth.

"This is nothing compared to what it will be like when I'm filling you."

I know he's just being sexy, but I can't help but hope he's saying this as a promise. If he's starting to believe our curses can be broken, maybe they will. The thought fills me with a new wave of pleasure. Winston's words, his touch, the hope—it's a perfect mixture of a feeling beyond this realm.

He focuses on my sensitive bud, flicking it up and down and increasing his tempo. "I want to taste you so bad. I want to put my lips around this bud."

"I'm close!" I yell.

"Come for me, baby." He whispers through gritted teeth as he bucks against my ass.

I want to touch him, to rub his hard length over his slacks, but he has me pinned, making it impossible to move, which is obviously a good thing. If I touch him like that, I'll die. The thought makes it so much more tempting, though.

I cry out as my body reaches its edge. The explosion of my orgasm crashes around me, but Winston doesn't remove any pressure, wringing out every last ounce of pleasure from me until my body slackens against him.

I catch my breath, resting against his hard chest. My head clears, and I realize the limo isn't moving.

The driver rolls down the divider a bit. "Sir, we've arrived."

I realize that it probably wasn't perfect timing. The driver waited for me to finish before he announced we'd reached our destination.

My cheeks heat. "I don't think the limo is that soundproof," I get out between labored breaths. I roll off Winston's lap.

Winston pulls off his white glove and licks his fingers, tucking his gloves in his pocket. His eyes roll back slightly as if my taste could bring him over the edge.

My core heats again at the sight.

"No, you were just very loud."

Chapter Seventeen

WINSTON

It takes me a second before I can step out of the limo.

Marigold watches me as I close my eyes and rest against my seat. I'm trying to think about anything but Marigold. I think of taxes, but then my mind wanders to Marigold naked and sprawled over my desk on top of tax forms. "Fuck." I moan.

"Are you okay?" Marigold asks, reaching over to push a strand of my hair back that came loose from my gel.

"God, don't touch me," I lean forward and press my head against the window.

"Sorry," she says softly.

I whip around back to her. "No, I'm sorry. I'm just trying not to think about you for a second."

She covers her mouth and giggles.

I smile. "Is this funny to you?"

"A little."

"Well, you better stop, or I'm going to kiss that smile right off your face." I turn and open the door.

"Go ahead. You'd die."

I lean into the limo and offer my hand to her. "Marigold, it would be an honor to die by your kiss."

Her cheeks heat, and I have to turn away. Damn, this will be a difficult journey, not even because we're negotiating with a vampire wizard with a reputation for being a dick.

"This is it?" Marigold asks as she stares at the dark warehouse building. She turns to look down the desolate street.

"Marigold, what did you think? There would be a big flashy sign that said *Magical Sex Club?*"

She shrugs. "I guess not."

I smile at her. "Most of these clubs aren't in magical communities like mine, so they must remain hidden."

She nods, and I take her hand and lead her to the metal door.

I knock.

A metal grate slides open at the top of the door. "Password?" says a gruff voice.

I lean in and whisper, "All good things happen after dark."

The metal grate closes, and the door swings open.

"How do you know the password?" Marigold whispers.

"All the magical sex clubs have the same one. It makes it easier."

I step inside, still holding Marigold's hand.

The room is dark, and all I can see is a large, dark figure with glowing eyes holding a candle. "Follow me," the figure orders.

This entrance differs from the clubs I've been to. Usually, you're greeted by a magical being who takes your coat and tells you to enjoy yourself. This feels a bit spooky. I don't say anything, though. I don't want to freak Marigold out.

The creature leads us through another door, spilling a low red light into the dark room. Once we enter, I can make out the minotaur who led us here. He is at least a foot taller than me, and I strain to look at his expression. His eyes are a lifeless black, and he seems more depressing than terrifying.

"Two?" asks a pale-faced woman at a black desk.

"Yes. I have an appointment with Draven. My name's Winston." G.M. told me she'd arrange an appointment with Draven for us. I hope their relationship isn't too tense for him to hate everyone with whom G.M. is associated. But G.M. wouldn't send us here if she knew it was hopeless. She must have some faith in him, even if she doesn't like the guy.

The woman flips through a black book, and I use her distraction to examine the room. Every club I've been in has low light—everything is less sinful in the dark—but the lighting here is such a dark red that it's suffocating. The walls have a strange wallpaper on them. I squint to get a better look and realize it's supposed to look like blood. Low music plays, but it can't cover the screams I hear in the distance. I hope those screams are from pleasure.

"Ah, yes. Here you are. He's expecting you." The dark-haired receptionist gets up from her seat and walks toward a set of doors.

I finally notice the fangs as she speaks.

I wonder if most people in this club are vampires, or it just so happens that it's owned by one and has a vampire receptionist. I don't particularly trust vampires. They're in the business of killing humans, and although I'm a wizard, I bleed just the same as everyone else. For once, I'm thankful for Marigold's curse. At least they can't hurt her. I grab Marigold's arm anyway. Even though she can protect herself, I feel better having her close.

"This place feels different," she whispers as we follow the vampire down a long, black hallway.

"I know. Stay close." I whisper back.

Doors line the walls on either side of us. Most of them seem to be occupied by the sounds that come from them, a mixture of pleasure and pain sends my hairs on their ends.

The hallway leads to a large room with a main stage, much like mine. The biggest difference—besides the more gothic feel—is the smaller stages around the room with long polls connecting to the ceiling. Girls dance half-naked on these poles. Some have obvious magical tells, while others look like regular humans. I try to catch their expressions to see if they're enjoying their jobs, but there's too much to see, and I'm trying to keep up with the receptionist.

On the main stage is a woman tied to an iron cross wearing a head-to-toe leather suit. A Centaur trots around her, whip in hand, and every few moments hits her with it. The audience holds many more men than women, and this sight unnerves me.

The sparse number of women in the crowd bounce up and down on the men's laps or pleasure the men on their knees.

I can't help but notice the men's eyes that follow Marigold. She's always a shining beacon, but in this dark place it's like she has a spotlight trailing her. I try to catch their eyes, daring one of them to try something.

The receptionist leads us to a door at the back of the large room. She opens it and signals for us to enter.

"Winston! I've heard so much about you!" The tall man behind the oak desk stands and walks toward us, waving his hand so the door we entered from shuts behind us. The low lights only accentuate his deathly pale skin. "I'm Draven. It's a pleasure to meet you." He offers his pale hand with long black fingernails. I must admit, he's a halfway decent-looking guy with dark hair and angular features. He must have turned when he was in his thirties.

I take his hand, shaking it firmly. "It's good to meet you, Draven." I motion behind me. "This is Marigold."

To my surprise, Marigold steps forward and offers her hand. "It's a pleasure to meet you." She drips with confidence. She's nothing like the timid woman I met just a few days ago. It warms my heart to see her feeling more comfortable in her skin, and I can't help but hope that I helped her achieve that.

Seeing her seemingly bare hand touch Draven does send an initial shock of surprise through my veins, but I remind myself it's an illusion dress. Her hands, as well as most of her body, remain covered.

Draven's expression shifts as he clasps her hand. I know when a man wants to gobble a woman up, and that's precisely what Draven is thinking. I clear my throat. "So, a wizard and a vampire, how did that happen?"

Draven shakes his head a little, knocking himself out of his trance. I can't say I blame him. Marigold is a heavenly creature. But she's mine, and he should know that.

I grab her by the waist, pulling her into me.

He waves his hand. "It's a boring story. I was born a wizard and got bit by a vampire later on. I'm surprised it doesn't happen to more of us, actually." He motions to the chairs in front of his desk. "Please come sit. I'll pour you both a drink."

"I heard that magical creatures' blood has a bitter taste for vampires," I say as we sit in the leather wingback chairs.

"That is true, but still. The perks are incredible. I'm much more powerful now than ever as a wizard."

I could argue with him about how that power comes with a price that any good-hearted person would never choose to make, but I don't have the time. I clear my throat. "I hate to cut to the chase, but we've heard that you could help us."

Draven's eyes trail over us, and he sighs before returning to his desk. He picks up a crystal glass and brings it to his lips. He watches us as he rests against his desk, licking the blood off his lips as he places his glass back on the desk. "Yes, you two want to break a curse."

"So, you can help us?" Marigold asks.

"Us? Are both of you cursed?" He asks, pouring red liquid into two crystal glasses and placing them before us. He turns and walks back behind his desk.

Marigold picks up her glass, but I signal with my eyes for her to put it down. I don't think she'd appreciate drinking human blood.

"Yes," I reply. "We're both cursed."

Draven smiles, revealing his white and pointy teeth. "How interesting." He leans forward, examining us before shaking his head. "I'm afraid I can't help you, though." He leans back and runs his hands through his jet-black hair.

"Why not?" Marigold leans forward in her chair, her face already hot with anger.

Draven widens his eyes and grins. "I don't know if you heard, but to cure your curse, you need to have virgin blood, and I doubt that's the case for either of you." He turns his attention to me. "You own a sex club in the magical community." He looks to Marigold. "And well... look at you." He smirks and sips his drink.

My blood boils, and I jump up from my chair, leaning over his desk. "Careful. I find it surprising that you so wrongly judge your guests. You'd think a vampire could read humans better. I guess you're not as powerful as they say."

"Winston." Marigold places her hand on my shoulder, and I turn to face her concerned expression. Her eyes remind me this is our only chance.

I clear my throat and straighten my lapels. "Excuse me," I mutter as I return to my seat.

Draven laughs and props his feet on his desk. "That was a good show, my boy. I can see your affections for the lady." He looks us over with a smile. "So, does your little outburst mean that the two of you are virgins?"

"Yes," Marigold replies.

I clench my jaw and keep my stare on Draven.

He gets up from his chair and paces around us. "Interesting." He leans in and sniffs Marigold.

"Watch it," I yell.

Marigold places her hand on my arm. "Winston, it's okay."

I examine her. Her eyes plead for me to stop. There's so much hope in them, and I can't disappoint her. But as I scan her body, I notice her dress is black. This isn't a color we originally discussed, but I can tell it means she's angry. I don't like this prick. I had a bad feeling from the moment we stepped into his club, but what other choice do I have but to sit here and hear him out? This is Marigold and I's only hope of being together.

"Now tell me, what are your curses?" He returns to his seat.

I can't bring myself to say another word to him, but thankfully, Marigold speaks up. "My touch turns people into gold. The witch who cursed my father's exact curse is, *For your greed will be rewarded with gold—a daughter's whose touch no mere mortal can ever hold.*" She turns to me as if asking if she should share mine.

I nod.

"Winston's is that he can't be intimate with someone. His curse is, *A touch for pleasure will reap pain. A mortal who indulges you, will be slain.*"

Draven taps his fingers against his lips. "Interesting. Your curses seem similar."

Marigold shrugs. "I guess, sort of."

"The language," Draven says. "It seems to be cast by the same witch. Of course, to learn how to break curses, I've had to study a lot about them. There's not that many witches, and they love having their own style regarding curses."

I lean forward in my chair. "What does that mean, our curses being from the same witch?"

Draven shrugs. "I'm not sure. Probably nothing, but it's curious that you two found each other. Maybe it's fate." He chuckles. "If you believe in that shit."

I do believe in that shit. To think that the woman both of our fathers crossed would be the same seems too serendipitous. I knew we were meant to be together, and this confirms it.

He clears his throat and sits on the edge of his desk before Marigold. "So, Marigold, quite a prophetic name, don't you think?"

When she doesn't respond, he goes on. "Have you ever tested out your curse?

Her eyes water and I'm about to interject when she responds, "Yes. My father was an evil man and used my curse to his advantage against my will."

Draven nods and rubs his chin. "But we shook hands earlier."

I speak. "She's wearing a magical illusion dress from Reginald's. Her skin is completely covered except her face."

He nods absent-mindedly, seeming lost in his thoughts.

I don't like the look on his face, as if he's decided the best way to eat her, but what else can I do without breaking Marigold's heart? Besides, I'd like to see him try to hurt her. She's too powerful.

"And you two? You care for each other, huh? That's why you're both here. So you can be together?" He returns to behind his desk, pacing with his hands behind his back.

"Yes," I proclaim proudly. "I love her. I'd do anything to be with her." My words shock me as much as the look on Marigold's face reads.

"You love me?" she whispers.

I shrug. "How could I not?"

She smiles, and her eyes light up. Her dress changes from black to bright yellow.

I don't even mind that she doesn't say it back immediately. This isn't the place where I thought I would reveal my love for Marigold, but I want Draven to know the truth. I am Marigold's, and she is mine.

"Well, isn't that precious?" Draven claps his hands with a smile. "I must say, I do not often see true love like this! Sure, I see plenty of sex, but that usually doesn't require love. You know what?" He snaps his fingers. "I like you two. Usually, I have a high price for breaking curses, but I'll help you both, free of charge."

"No, that won't be necessary. Name your price. We can pay it." I don't like the idea of being indebted to this guy.

"Please, it's no bother! It'd be my honor to bring together you two star-crossed lovers. Of course, the process will take several hours, so it's best that the two of you stay overnight."

"Overnight?" I ask skeptically.

"I can promise we'd provide the most comfortable lodgings. Why don't you follow me and I'll show you to our facilities? We'll get started right away on extracting your blood. Unless that is, you want to enjoy the club for the rest of the night?" He gives a devilish grin.

Usually, the thought of enjoying a magical sex club would thrill me, especially after touching Marigold in the limo, but since entering the club, I've sobered up. I don't think I'd like the activities they partake in, and I think Marigold would enjoy them even less. I scan Marigold to see what her dress shows. It's a light blue, telling me my intuition was spot on.

I speak up. "We're good. We want to break this curse as soon as possible."

Draven nods. "Suit yourself, although Marigold would be quite a hit on that main stage."

I must admit the thought of Marigold on a stage naked for all to see with her hands deep in her cunt pleasuring herself, just like I taught her, sends a thrill down my spine. But then I remembered that men would stare at her, and I sobered back up. Who would have thought I could turn into such a prude? But I want Marigold all to myself.

Draven shrugs and presses a button on his desk when we don't reply. "Esmerelda, please send the trolls to my office. I need their help directing our guests to the lab."

The lab? It sounds so modern—nothing like I'd expect for a vampire sex club.

The door swings open within seconds, and two monstrous trolls duck inside.

I wonder why he'd need them to escort us to the lab, but Draven walks between them out to the club before I can ask. "Follow me," he yells back to us.

The trolls follow behind him, and Marigold and I are alone for a moment.

I stand and grab Marigold's hand. We catch each other's gaze. I can't read her expression or the color of her dress. She seems to have a mix of hopefulness and fear.

"You ready?" I ask.

She nods, and we turn to follow Draven and the trolls.

The club is just as depressing and dark as when we arrived, except now it seems even more crowded with men in sleek suits. As I look closer, I realize almost all of them are vampires, with thirst in their eyes as they stare up at the women performers. I don't like it one bit, but there's nothing I can do right now. Not when Marigold and I have a curse to break.

Draven stops and turns to us. "I have some business to attend to in the club. I'm sure you understand, Winston. My security here will direct you to the blood collection room." He waves before disappearing through the crowd of men.

I clench Marigold's hand tighter as we follow the trolls through several hallways and up numerous flights of stairs. We're finally led to a sterile white room with a single chair in the middle.

"You stay here," one of the trolls says as he motions to me.

"You come with me," says the other troll, motioning to Marigold.

Marigold flashes me a look of terror, and I hold her hand tighter. "No, we stay together."

"Only one chair here to collect blood. She must go to another room." The first troll protests.

I turn to Marigold, searching her face. "I'll do whatever you want to do. Just say the word, and we'll ditch this place."

Marigold shakes her head. "No, this is our only hope. I'll be okay."

Her eyes and the dark blue dress does nothing to convince me. But what more can I say, to Marigold? This is our only chance at being together.

"Okay." I walk into the sterile room.

"Nurse will be here soon," the troll says before slamming the door.

I rush toward it, turning the handle. Panic seeps into my veins when I realize it's locked. This isn't good. Why would they need to lock me in this room? I take my wand out of my pocket and flick it toward the doorknob, but nothing happens when I turn it again. They must have cast a spell on this door, so my magic would be useless. Shit, this is bad.

I bang on the door because it's the only thing I can do.

Marigold screams from across the hall, and my whole world shatters.

CHAPTER EIGHTEEN

MARIGOLD

I never make it to my collection room. The trolls grab me by my arms and carry me down another hallway. I scream, hoping one of them will try to cover my mouth and turn to gold, but they must know they shouldn't because they continue to carry me without touching my exposed skin. Draven must have whispered something to them during those few seconds Winston and I were left alone in his office.

Winston. All I can think about is Winston. What did they do with him? I struggle against the trolls' grips, knowing that if I could remove my glove, I could save us both. But the trolls' strengths are no match for me.

They carry me to a wing that looks more like a medieval dungeon than part of a modern magical sex club. The flooring and walls are all natural stone, with candles creating a dim light and metal bars caging in small rooms. Draven seriously needs some interior design help. He has like five different eras going on in his club slash lab slash dungeon. Actually, he probably just needs a lobotomy.

They throw me onto the floor in one of the cells, and the wind is knocked out of me. It takes me a second to regain my breath, but I charge toward the bars once I do. "Let me out!" I yell, even though I know it's futile.

The trolls watch me and chuckle. "What a shame we can't enjoy this one for ourselves," one troll says to the other, drool dripping from his mangled fangs.

The other leers at me. "I know we're not supposed to touch her skin, but I can think of some ways those pretty little hands can make themselves useful."

"Fuck you!" I yell before spitting on them through the bars. "Where's Winston?"

The trolls laugh harder. "Aw, the little lady misses her weak little wizard. How cute. This is going to be a fun one to break."

"I'd like to see either of you try!" I yell.

One of the trolls, the tallest and the one covered with the most warts, closes the gap between us, his putrid breath just inches from my face. "I'd watch it, missy. This is going to be your home for the rest of your life. It can either be a fun experience or a treacherous one. You may not know because of that weak wizard you spent time with, but Draven can cause you extreme pain without touching a pretty little hair on your head."

I think of the extreme pleasure Winston gave me with his magic, and I shiver thinking about how the opposite can very well be true. I fight back the tears pushing at the back of my eyes, clenching my fists to focus on a different type of pain. "What does he want with me?" Surely, it can't be for his physical enjoyment. I'd kill him unless he really can break my curse, which I don't believe is true now.

The trolls laugh again, and I decide their laughter has to be the worst thing I've ever heard. "Poor, dumb little girl."

"It's your touch, stupid," the troll farther away says between laughs. "You can turn people into gold. You're a powerful weapon and will make Draven one wealthy man."

Panic rises through me. How could I be so stupid? My own father used me for power and wealth. How could I not predict that a stranger with a bad reputation wouldn't do the same thing?

I want to cry and roll up in a ball in the corner of my cell, but then I remember everything that's changed within me in the last few days. I'm not the timid little girl I used to be. Just like I did with my father, I can defeat these bastards. They want to use my powers against me? Well, good luck to them because I sure as hell will make sure it's the last thing they do.

My powers are no different than they were before, but I'm different, and I'm in love. The realization washes over me like a tidal wave. I'm in love with Winston and don't care if Draven is a fraud and can't break our curses. I can't believe it takes something as dramatic as both of us getting kidnapped for me to admit it to myself.

Nothing in life is guaranteed, and I need to enjoy every second I have with Winston while I can. And I plan to do just that once I get us both out of here. Sure, he's a powerful wizard, but so is Draven. Winston is just one man against Draven's army. He needs me.

First, I need to come up with a plan for how to get ourselves out of here. The first step in that plan is making these trolls think they broke me. I decide to follow through with my initial instinct. I crumble to the floor, wrapping my arms around my knees and bellowing sobs.

"Aw, you made the little lady cry," one of the trolls says.

"Such a pity. Maybe she'll realize that working with us is the best thing she can do. You know, little golden lady, if you just use that tiny little hand of yours to stroke my cock, I can ensure you're treated like a queen here. Draven told us that your magical dress covers them."

I try to focus on holding the bile back in my throat and resist the urge to tell them both to fuck themselves, but then an idea pops into my head. What if these two idiots are my ticket out? I can play along, even if it makes me want to vomit my guts out. I won't have to go very far. All I need is the opportunity to get within reach of them.

I pick my head up, puckering my lips and bulging my eyes. "I'm so hungry. Can I get something to eat?"

"See, Igor." The larger troll turns to the smaller one. "Women like to act all big and tough until any small thing bothers them." He turns back to me. "You want some food, little one? Okay, but it's gonna cost you."

He really must be an idiot to think he can bride me with food when I've only been captured for less than twenty minutes. But idiots are good. Idiots mean I can get out of here easily.

The smaller one clears his throat. "Bork, do you think Draven would like us messing with his prisoner?"

Bork waves his hand in refusal. "Ah, he doesn't have to know about this. He'll be busy for the rest of the night. We can have our fun, and he'll never know about it."

Igor shrugs. "If you say so."

"Come on, let's get the prisoner food, and then we'll have some fun!" Bork winks at me before turning to leave the dungeon.

Finally, I'm alone with my thoughts, so I can figure out a plan to get out of here. I'm not sure how much time I have before they return, but if I learned anything about those two bumbling idiots in the last few minutes, even making a sandwich would be difficult for them. I've got plenty of time.

Chapter Nineteen

MARIGOLD

It takes thirty minutes for Bork and Igor to return. They don't even have a sandwich, just a bag of chips and a granola bar. Do they really think I'll give them a hand job for that? God, maybe Draven's the bigger idiot for hiring these two.

"Thank God, I'm starving," I say, throwing myself against the bars. I've transformed my dress so that it's nothing but lingerie. A tight bustier covers my midriff, and my boobs spill out of the top. My bottoms are cheeky underwear attached to garters and high socks.

Droll spills from the corners of both of their mouths.

As much as I hate presenting myself this way for these dickwads, I know showing more skin will distract them even more.

"What happened to your dress?" Igor asks.

I trail my hands up my body, keeping my expression soft and pouty. "It's a magical dress, remember? I can make it look like anything I want, but every inch of my skin is covered."

Bork chuckles and walks closer to the cage.

Igor scrunches his crusty lips and stays put. "How do we know you didn't take your dress off?"

I bat my eyelashes. "Well, do you see any dress in this dungeon? I'm the only thing here, and I'm just so hungry and want to do whatever I can to get some food." Internally, I cringe. I'm not a good actress, and obviously, my motives for transforming into a starved bimbo within five minutes aren't believable. But I hope these trolls have as few brain cells as I predict and that my tits look good enough to distract the remaining ones.

"Come on, Igor, let's check out the cell. I'll go in, and you can stand outside the door just to be safe."

Shit. My plan rests entirely on them both being in here with the cell door open.

"I was thinking I could pleasure you both at the same time." I move my hands as if I'm jacking off imaginary dicks. "That way, we can get this done faster if your master comes down."

Their eyes stay firmly locked on my motions.

I think I finally killed their last two brain cells because they both enter the cell, leaving the door ajar.

"See, no extra clothing around here." I bat my eyelashes as they approach me, my hands behind my back.

Leering smiles take up half of their faces, revealing their decayed and half-missing teeth. They both kneel in front of me. Their eyes are glazed in a delirious state, and the sight of it sends a surge of power through my veins.

This plan isn't a good one. Most *people* would never agree to get into a cage with a dangerous and captured girl, but my ability to lure these men to their deaths with just my words and sex appeal makes me feel like a powerful siren.

Both trolls fumble with their pants, looking down to unbuckle their belts.

I have no interest in witnessing smelly troll dick. I move quickly, placing my hands on both of their arms.

I stand before them, watching them scream and look up at me with wide eyes. They reach for me, but I step back, smiling as I watch their skin become gold.

"You bitch," Bork gargles before his mouth freezes.

"God, it pays to have magical gloves." I sigh and pick the gloves off the floor where they've rested invisibly, shaking the apparent nothingness in their line of vision.

"Igor, Bork, is everything all right?" a voice calls from somewhere far away.

"'Shit," I whisper to myself, running past the now golden troll statues and pushing open the cell door.

Now that I'm free and gloveless, no one can stop me. Without hesitation, I charge toward the hall I came from until I reach three men, presumably vampires by their pale skin.

"Hey, how did you get out?" one of them says as he charges toward me, clearly not knowing what I'm capable of or adrenaline making him forget.

I charge toward them, my arms outstretched. I grab one of the men's arms, and he freezes with a groan. I don't stop to watch him transform and continue down the line until I've turned all three men into pillars of gold.

It was so effortless. It barely took ten seconds to kill three vampires with a simple touch. I look down at my hands, shaking. I've always hated my curse more than anything, but now power surges through me. I alone can protect the people I love. The thought of Winston snaps me out of my trance, and I run down the hallway the trolls took me through.

I get to the door of the room where I saw Winston last. I don't know if he stayed in this room or was moved elsewhere. My heart beats out of my chest as I think of the possibility that it's too late. I grab the handle. Luckily, the door is unlocked, and I swing it open.

"Winston," I yell. He's here. My heart sings.

He stands inches from me, his wand pointed at my face.

His eyes seem to register that it's me and not a threat. "Marigold," he yells before dropping his arm and moving toward me, his face alight with relief.

"Wait, don't touch me."

He looks down at my body. I hadn't had a chance to think about transforming my dress back to its original form.

"What happened?" His face heats, and I'm unsure if it's with desire or anger. Maybe a mixture of both.

"I had to distract the trolls to get close to touch them. I'm wearing the same dress, but I lost my gloves." I must have lost them in the tussle with the vampires.

"Are you okay?" He moves as if to touch me, and I step back.

"Yes, I'm fine. Are you okay?" It's so good to see him. I want to tell him how much I love him and that I don't care if my curse will never be broken. We can find a way to be together. But now's not the time. Now, we need to get the hell out of here.

He nods. "Yeah, I'm good. They must have put a spell on the door to make it impossible to use magic to get out from the inside." His expression turns downward. "Marigold, I'm so sorry. I can't believe I let this happen to you." He runs his fingers through his hair. "I couldn't get out of this fucking room to save you."

I wish I could touch him. "Winston, it's okay. I'm fine. I'm the one who wanted to come here. I knew the risk."

A sound like a door banging open bellows down the hall, and I get my mind back on track. "We need to go."

I'm hoping he has a plan to get out of here because finding him was as far as I got.

Luckily, he speaks. "We need to find a window and try to climb down. If we go down the stairs, someone will catch us."

"I can take them."

"I know you can, but it's the safest way. Someone could have a gun and wouldn't need to get close to you to take you down." He reaches for me as if the thought alone makes him want me closer. "Let's go." He peeks out the door. "We're clear."

We both run into the hall, charging in the opposite direction of the increasing sounds. We pass the dungeon area where I was held and the vampires I turned to gold just moments before. The walls change from natural stone back to concrete. Sure enough, there's a window at the end of the hallway.

Winston pries open the window and looks down. "There's a fire escape." He pulls himself out, and I follow.

"He's gone!" The echo of someone yelling down the long hallway is the last thing I hear before Winston pulls the window shut. "Go," he whispers.

I rush down the stairs. My heart beats out of my chest. It's so dark, and I'm only worried about getting out of here. I don't even notice the rusty metal that makes up the fire escape or the gaping hole where a step should be.

I scream as I fall, bracing myself for my untimely death, but I don't meet the ground. Something stopped me.

I open my eyes and look down to see my feet dangling from at least four stories. I look up to see what kept me from falling.

Winston is grabbing my arm.

Winston is touching my bare skin.

Our eyes meet, and my earth shatters.

CHAPTER TWENTY

WINSTON

It was worth it. My instincts told me to grab Marigold from falling to her death, but now that I'm staring down at her, watching the tears well in her eyes, I know I would make this choice a million times over. Marigold is worth everything in this world, even my life. I can't think of a better way to die than by saving the other piece of my soul.

"It's okay," I whisper, pulling her up. I don't know how long it will take for the transformation to happen, but her skin radiates under my touch. Something is happening.

"Winston, no!" She cries, pulling herself up the rest of the way and looking me over with frantic, tear-soaked eyes.

I reach out and touch her cheek. If these are my last moments, I want them to be spent touching her skin. It's just as soft as I imagined, but the energy buzzing between us is far greater than anything I've ever experienced.

"Marigold, it's okay." I smile at her, pulling her close. I've been dreaming of the taste of her lips. Why haven't I touched her sooner? Sure, I'm about to die, but this is all worth it. Speaking of dying, isn't that supposed to happen soon? Maybe it will take a while, which is fine by me. If I'm going to die, I want the last thing I do to be kissing Marigold.

I grab the back of her neck, pulling her into me. I think the transformation is happening because the moment our lips touch, every nerve in my body ignites.

She's stiff at first, even pulling back slightly, but I don't let go, letting my tongue drag over the seam of her lips. Her body slackens, and she falls into me, opening her lips and allowing me to taste her.

God, this is heaven. Maybe I'm already dead, and this will be how I spend the rest of eternity.

My hands move from her neck to down her back. I'm ravenous, wanting to touch every inch of her before it's too late, but my exploration halts when she pulls back.

"Winston, wait." She touches my face. Her eyes are frantic as she examines me. "You're....you're not turning." She backs away from me, looking at my hands and then back to my eyes. "What do you feel?"

"I feel alive. For the first time." I'm drunk off her taste and lean forward, wanting more.

"Winston, no. Wait. You should be gold already. Why aren't you gold?" Tears fall from her cheek.

Her words momentarily knock me out of my lovestruck trance, and I look down at myself. She's right. I should be turning. There's no way she got away from the trolls if it took this long for her touch to go into effect. "I... I don't know. But I'm not turning." I look up at her, my head spinning with a mixture of confusion and pure joy.

"Hey! Maybe they went out here!" yells a voice from overhead as someone opens the window we escaped from.

"Come on! We have to go." I grab Marigold's hand. Her bare hand, and God, does it feel magnificent. I lead her down the fire escape as the voices grow louder behind us. I jump to the street, my arms outstretched to catch Marigold.

"Hey, there they are!" a dark figure yells from two stories above us on the fire escape.

"Let's get out of here." I grab Marigold's hand, and we run toward the front of the building.

The limo's still there waiting for us, and I open the door, pushing Marigold in before I jump inside and slam the door behind me. "Go!" I yell to the driver.

Hands bang on the back of the limo as we pull away.

I exhale. We're safe for now. I turn to Marigold, and she's already watching me. "You're alive," she gets out breathlessly.

I grab her hand. "Finally."

Chapter Twenty-One

MARIGOLD

My head spins as we enter the hotel room. It hasn't stopped since Winston grabbed my hand on the fire escape. My lips are still numb from his kiss—the first kiss I've ever experienced, but I know it wasn't normal. I think when romance novels and movies describe kisses as being electric, they're being poetic. But the kiss Winston and I had was literally electric, in the best way possible.

I sit on the edge of my bed, looking down at my hands—the hands that killed so many people but, for some reason, didn't kill Winston.

Winston and I haven't said a word since we got into the limo, which is odd, but especially because we should be all over each other now that we know we can touch. Not only touch, kiss. Wouldn't a kiss be considered intimate? Does that mean that Winston's curse is broken, too? But maybe not. How can we be sure that if anything else happened between us, I wouldn't die? My body buzzes with anticipation. Knowing that I can't kill Winston, I don't think I'd mind risking my life to test if his curse could still affect me. I'm confused, wondering what we should do or say next.

Winston's pacing before me, looking down at his feet as if deep in thought.

We should talk this out. Maybe we can figure out what's going on and our next steps. I breathe out, parting my lips to speak, but before any words leave my mouth, Winston breaks the distance between us. He grabs the back of my head, pulling my lips to his, before pressing his weight against me and pushing me back against the bed.

The same electricity I felt the first time we kissed pulsates at every spot he touches.

He pulls back and looks at the spot where his hand is on my arm. "Do you feel that?"

I nod. "I felt it when you touched me the first time. What is it?"

"I think it's our curses counteracting each other." He runs his finger down my arm.

I throw my head back. "God, it feels good."

He leans forward, capturing my lips again. His hands explore more of my skin. The electricity sends shocks of pleasure at every place he touches—my body hums with need.

He pulls back, his breath heavy as he yanks at my dress, trying to pull my straps down. My dress is still in its lingerie form, but Winston rips it off me, pulling it down my ankles so I'm bare.

"Winston," I say in more of a moan.

"If you want me to stop, tell me now because I can't wait another second to explore every inch of you."

I should tell him to stop, even though I'm already naked. We should take this slow and talk about the possibilities and the near-death we just escaped, but my words betray my rational thoughts. "Don't stop."

Winston presses his lips to mine again, his hands trailing down my neck and reaching my chest. He picks his head up, "God, you taste so fucking good." He looks down at my body. "Fuck," he turns away. "Marigold, this is too much."

"Take your clothes off," I beg. "I want to feel you against me." God, do I want to feel him. I want to grip his impressive length before he thrusts it inside me. The fear that maybe his curse isn't broken and that this could end my life isn't anywhere in my thoughts. He's right, for some reason, our curses are counteracting each other. That must be what the vibrations are when we touch and why neither of us is dead yet. We've defied all odds. His hands are all over my naked body, and he's still whole. For whatever reason, it confirms my suspicions all along. We're meant for each other. We're two parts of a whole and about to be complete. Not even witches, curses, vampires, or death could part us.

He pulls up and unbuttons his shirt, revealing his chiseled body.

I want to reach forward and run my hands down his muscles, but he's moving quickly, taking off his belt and pulling down his slacks. Before I have time to sit up and touch him, he's lunging forward, pressing his hard body against mine and kissing my lips. He's still wearing his form-fitting boxers, but I feel his length rubbing against me.

He kisses down my neck until he gets to my breasts. He laps at my nipple as he grabs my other breast and rubs his thumb back and forth.

"Winston," I cry. "It's too good." I feel myself getting closer to that edge from his mouth on me.

He looks up at me, and I catch his dark and hungry gaze. "There's no such thing as too good. Don't be afraid to come for me, baby. I've got all the time in the world and plan to make you keep coming all night."

His words send a shiver down my spine, and I throw my head back with a moan.

He crawls down my body, leaving a trail of kisses in his wake. "God, I can't tell you how much I dreamed about this. I'm still unsure if I'm dead, and this is heaven." He crawls onto the floor, grabbing my legs and pulling me to him. He spreads my legs apart and looks down at me before pressing a single kiss to my bare cunt. "Yes, heaven exists between your legs."

God, the buzz from his lips on my core is almost too much. I can't imagine anything being better than this feeling. He's right. This has to be heaven. There's no other explanation for how this can feel so good.

This is our first time fully together. I want to make it last, but that probably won't happen. It feels like I have a lifetime's worth of pent-up attraction to Winston, and now that he's started, the floodgates will burst open.

He picks me up, gripping my ass and bringing me to his lips. He lightly kisses my seam until I'm squirming in his grip. He dips his tongue in, slowly licking me up and down.

I clench the sheets next to me, letting the moans of my ecstasy roll over me.

"Oh my God, Marigold. You taste so fucking good." He licks up and down, increasing his tempo until I'm quivering. He focuses on my clit, rolling his tongue over it and then sucking it lightly.

Stars cloud my vision, and I grab Winston's hair as my orgasm washes over me.

He doesn't let up until my body goes limp, but nothing is sated within me. If anything, I want more. I will never be satisfied until he's deep within me, and even then, I don't think it would be enough.

I reach for him. "Please, I need you."

His eyes are heated, and my moisture dampens his lips. He crawls over me, and I grab his neck, pulling him into me. The taste of myself on his lips ignites a moan from the back of my throat. I reach down under the waistband of his boxers, grasping for him.

The moment my fingers touch his length, a harsh hiss escapes from him, and he freezes. He captures my gaze, his eyes an intense stare. I can feel his heartbeat drumming wildly.

"Are you okay?" I ask, still gripping him.

He nods, his lips pressed together. "Are you okay?" He studies me.

"Yes. As you said, our curses counteract each other for some reason. I'm fine." I begin to work my hand down, and he softly moans. "I want this. No matter what it means. We're meant to be together." I continue stroking him up and down, lathering my palm in the precum that gathers at his tip.

"I love you, Marigold," he says, and the sound of his labored words makes my toes curl. It's not the first time he's said it, but it feels like it. I imagine that every time I hear those words leave his lips, my heart will flutter as if it's the first. I'll never get enough of it.

"I love you, Winston." I love him. I love him. If we're horribly wrong and Winston's curse isn't quite broken, I'm glad these will be my last words. But I know that's not the case. Here I am, stroking him, feeling as he pulses with each movement. We're as intimate as can be. Well, of course, until he's inside of me.

He leans down to kiss me while working his boxers completely off him. Now we're both bare, and he presses his body against mine. I could roll around like this all day, feeling his skin. The skin I've always dreamed of touching. But then his fingers trail down the side of my body, searching for the heat between my legs, and I know I want more. I want all of him.

He sticks a finger inside of me. "You're so wet. Are you going to come for me again?" He strokes up and down, his finger gliding through me.

"I need you inside of me, now," I beg.

My words send a shiver down his body as he positions the head of his cock at my entrance. "I'll go slow. I don't want to hurt you," he whispers.

My hands tangle in his wavy hair as he slowly thrusts into me. Pain shoots up my body, and I give a small cry.

"Are you okay?" he asks, searching my face.

I nod. "Don't stop." I want more of him. I want all of him, and this small fraction of my pain is nothing compared to this want seeping out of me.

He works more of himself into me. With each inch, the pain lessens, and the pleasure fills its void.

I tug at Winston's hair and moan.

He looks up at me, his gaze burning into me as he increases his speed. He presses himself against me without stopping his thrusts, kissing down my neck before bringing his lips to my ear. "Marigold," he moans.

I've always loved the sound of my name on his lips, and he's so good at continuously saying it. But hearing my name right now, as he pumps deep inside of me, hitting a spot deep within me that ignites my body—my name has never sounded sweeter.

His speed increases even more, and my name falls off his lips as if he's in a trance. "Marigold, Marigold, Marigold."

Another wave of pleasure rushes through me, and my body tenses. My second orgasm is as great as the first, if not better, because this time, Winston is coming with me.

He cries out as he empties himself within me, his warmness filling me. "Fuck!" he cries.

My hands are still tangled in his hair, and his lips are still pressed against my neck until our bodies finally slacken, and the only sound in the room is our labored breaths.

As my body relaxes, the realization of what just happened and the weight of Winston's body on mine hits me. I bring consciousness to all parts of my body. Everything feels fine. Well, much better than fine.

Winston's eyes are closed, and his head rests against mine. His chest rises and falls on top of me.

We're alive. More alive than I ever thought was possible.

Chapter Twenty-Two

WINSTON

The sun shines through the crack in the white curtains of Marigold's hotel room, illuminating a sliver of her angelic face. I prop up on my elbow, grab my glasses from the bedside table, and look down at her as she sleeps. Our legs are intertwined, and her ass is pressed against my morning wood. I don't dare wake her and make my way inside her again. Our first time together wasn't our last for the night. Marigold must be exhausted from the three separate times we made love. I don't think I could ever get tired of being deep inside her or having my tongue between her legs, but I don't want to tire Marigold out so soon.

She needs her sleep, and I don't mind letting her do so while I watch the rise and fall of her chest, in awe that this beautiful woman is mine. Finally, completely mine.

I would have spent the rest of my life loving Marigold from a distance, getting our fix of each other however we could—but God, the connection we felt last night, makes life heavenly. I'm mentally kicking myself that we could have been experiencing the bliss of each other so much sooner, but I guess the waiting and anticipation made our connection even stronger.

My mind whirls with the words from our curses and how they could possibly work against each other. Draven did say that the same witch made our curses. Maybe that alone cancels each other out. Or perhaps it has to do with the words "mortal" in each of our curses. Neither of us is completely mortal, technically. I'm a magical wizard, and she's a powerful enchantress with a magical touch. Maybe we are as otherworldly as I predicted and destined by the Gods for one another.

I know Marigold's curse isn't broken. She killed the trolls that captured her and the vampires that stood in her way. I doubt my curse is broken, either. Our curses make us immune to the other's curse, and for some reason, that's even more exciting than our curses being broken altogether. No one can touch her except me, and Marigold will be the only person I'm with for the rest of my life.

If only we didn't bother wasting our time with Draven. Although, I don't know if we'd ever figured out the loophole to our curses without the threat of death that Draven gave us.

G.M. Fairy said she didn't get along with Draven. I doubt she would send us to him if she knew just how evil he is. Maybe the people he truly wronged never had a chance to tell it? Maybe no one knows just how evil he is. Well, the ignorance of Draven's wickedness ends now. I'll spread the message and take up an army to ensure his power is stripped from him. But first, we need to get the hell out of the city and back to Florida, where Marigold is safe.

Marigold needs her rest before our journey. I'll let her sleep for a few more hours and go downstairs to get her some breakfast. She's never had New York bagels before. I can't let her leave New York City without experiencing New York bagels.

I crawl out of bed, careful not to stir Marigold, and slip out of the room.

***

I make my way back to the golden elevator at the back of the hotel, juggling the bag of bagels and the drink carrier full of coffee, creamer, and sugar. I hope Marigold is still sleeping so I can steal a few more minutes of watching her. We've got our whole lifetime ahead of us, but it doesn't make me any less eager to hold on to all of the simple moments with her as I can.

The elevator doors open to the seventh floor, and I fumble, trying to retrieve my key from my pocket. I swing the door open, looking down at the breakfast to make sure everything is still intact.

The hairs on the back of my neck stand up. Something isn't right. My eyes haven't adjusted to the room's darkness, but when I flip the light switch on, I see Marigold with a gloved hand over her mouth and a gun pointed at her head.

The contents drop from my hands, and I dart to the bedside table to grab my wand.

"Don't move a muscle, or her pretty little brains will be splattered all over the wall."

I freeze, meeting the gaze of the man who walks from the shadows in the corner of the room. Draven.

"If you kill her, I imagine she wouldn't be much use to you," I get out through gritted teeth. I look up at Marigold, tears flooding her hazel eyes.

The man with a gloved hand over Marigold's mouth wears a full-body suit, and another man wearing the same suit, grabs her hands behind her back and snaps on a pair of handcuffs.

Marigold's muffled sobs sink a dagger through my heart. She's still naked. So much of her powerful skin is exposed, but it means nothing to these men who have done all they can to protect themselves from her.

Draven chuckles and walks closer to Marigold, running a gloved finger up and down her bare arm. "She's either dead or making me the richest man ever to exist." Draven flips toward me, pointing his wand in my direction.

My feet lift from the ground, and invisible hands grasp my throat. "Of course, I'd much rather be wealthy, so I'll take you as collateral."

I claw at his power around my neck, feeling helpless as my vision tunnels.

Marigold wiggles her mouth free from her captor's hands. "Please, stop! I'll do what you want. Just don't hurt him!"

"That's more like it!" Draven booms. The grip around my neck loosens. "Now, we can all work together to make this a mutually beneficial deal. Of course, it won't be your initial plan where you two are free of your curses and go back home to live your happily ever after, but I think you both would be quite pleased to keep the other alive." He straightens his black suit and runs his pale hand through his jet-black hair. "Now then, let's get back to my place and we can sort this all out together."

I make one last attempt to dart toward my wand with all my might, but it's futile. When I'm just in reach, Draven points his wand toward me, and a force slams into my head.

"Winston, no!" Marigold's voice is the last thing I hear.

Chapter Twenty-Three

WINSTON

I wake to a metal door slamming in the distance and rub at my temples. Everything is blurry, so I know I'm not wearing my contacts. I feel around on the cold stone floor I'm lying on until my fingers graze my glasses.

I put them on and sit up. "Fuck," I moan, my head pounding even worse. I take in my surroundings as I get a handle on my pain. I'm in a cell of a dungeon. The events from before I was knocked out flood my memory.

I jump to my feet and grab the metal bars of my cage. "Marigold!" I yell in desperation. I instinctually pat my pockets, praying to the universe that I might have been taken with my wand. "Shit," I mutter, realizing my luck has run out.

I scream, shaking the bars with all my might until a wave of despair washes over me, and I fall to the floor, resting my head in my hands.

I'd had everything. I thought my life was about to fall into the sweet bliss of happily ever after, but how could I be so stupid? Of course, Draven would come after us.

Just as I'm about to give in to my hopelessness, my will sucker punches me in the gut. No. I will get out of here with Marigold if it's the last thing I do. This is our destiny. What kind of destiny would we have if it ended with me rotting in a cell and Marigold living a life as a slave? This can't be the end of our story.

I get to my feet, ready to derive a plan, when footsteps echo closer.

I shoot my attention to the hallway at the room's far end. Two tall vampires walk toward me, their eyes dark as night contrasting their sickly pale skin. "You're coming with us." One of them says as he pulls out a brass key to open my cage.

"And don't think about trying anything. We're taking you to Marigold, so you better comply," the other says as he reaches in and grabs my arm.

I yank back against his grip, but he holds on tighter. Vampires have the power of unusual strength. There's no hope of getting away from them without my wand.

Although my heart lightens that I'm being taken to Marigold, dread fills the back of my mind. Draven wouldn't take me to see Marigold unless it were to get her to do something for him. This can't be good.

I'm brought down flights of stairs onto the club's main floor. I'm guessing it's still the middle of the day because the place is barren. The fluorescent lights flicker overhead, revealing all the club's hidden corners. There's a hunched-back elf mopping up a large puddle of blood, and the whole space smells of death and sex.

A shiver runs down my spine. I can't believe I brought Marigold here, thinking it would be the answer to our prayers. Darkness covers sins, but in the light, this place is as disgusting as I felt in my bones.

The vampires take me to Draven's office. My head swivels around the room until I find Marigold.

She's seated at the same chair she sat the first time we came here.

The vampires led me to the chair beside her.

I lean forward to catch Marigold's expression. Her posture is ridged, and her gaze remains straight ahead.

"Marigold," I whisper. I need to look into her eyes and know that she's okay.

The large chair behind the oak desk swivels to face us. "She's under my magic. She can't move." Draven smiles at us, clacking his black fingernails against a crystal orb in his hands.

I search for Marigold's eyes again and watch a tear fall down her cheek.

My mind wracks for how to get us out of here. Draven must have brought us to his office for a reason. Maybe I can negotiate.

"What do you want with me?" I ask.

Draven throws his head back and laughs. "I don't want anything with you. What use could I have for another weakling wizard?" He picks up my wand from his desk. "You can't even perform magic without your little friend right here."

My wand is here in the room with us. I could lunge forward and grab it, but I don't want to risk anything while Marigold is under his power.

I clear my throat. "Then, why am I still alive?"

"Good question." Draven stands and walks to the other side of his desk, resting in front of us. "Marigold here has been very difficult the past few hours. Of course, I can use magic to freeze her, but it exerts my powers. I can't continue to freeze her like this to get her to turn people into gold."

Good. I hope Marigold puts up such a fight that he's completely depleted by his greed.

"That's where you come in." Draven points to me. "If we threaten to torture you. She'll do whatever we ask. Draven jumps to his seat in one swift movement, and his fist meets my jaw.

I taste blood, and my head sags to the side.

Marigold whimpers from next to me.

Draven snaps his fingers, and I hear Marigold move from next to me.

"Winston!" she cries as she gets up from her chair and steps toward me.

"Stop right there," Draven orders, pointing a finger at Marigold. "If you don't sit your pretty little ass back down and do as I say, the next thing you'll hear is his cries as I slice one of his fingers off."

Marigold sniffles as she sits back in her seat.

Draven runs his fingers through his hair, seeming to release tension in his scalp. "Besides, you wouldn't want to be foolish and accidentally touch him. If you turn him into a statue of gold, I bet you'd be pretty upset." He taps his finger against his lip. "Although, maybe if you had nothing to live for, you'd comply more."

Draven doesn't know we're able to touch. Marigold and I had grabbed hands as we ran to the limo after escaping, but maybe his men didn't register what happened or the news never got back to him.

My mind races with how we could use this information to defeat him, but right now, he doesn't want me to turn into a statue of gold. He wants to keep me alive to get Marigold to comply.

Draven's voice knocks me out of my trance. "Bring her in," he yells to someone on the other side of his office door.

The door swings open and in walks two vampires carrying an unconscious woman. One of the vampires grabs a chair up against the wall, and they both place the woman in it.

My stomach drops. I know exactly where this is going.

Draven clears his throat. "Marigold, it's time for your first act of service. The first one will always be the hardest, but I promise it will get easier." Draven turns to his desk to retrieve his drink.

"No!" Marigold stands from her chair and charges toward Draven.

A pain radiates through my head, and I cry out, folding forward.

"Winston!" Marigold yells and rushes toward me.

"Remember, you act out of line, and Winston suffers." Draven calmly sips his drink, keeping his back to Marigold.

Marigold returns to her seat and the pain in my head subsides.

Draven places his drink on the desk and turns to us. "Now, I hope we're seeing things clearly. Marigold, you'll touch that woman in the chair over there. She's a nobody. She's a dried-out hooker nobody cares about spending time with in the club. No one will miss her. Touch her, and your work will be finished for the night, and Winston won't have to suffer anymore."

"Marigold, don't do this!" I yell. I'll suffer all the pain in the world to give her freedom.

Draven sends another wave of pain through my head, and I double over.

"That's enough talk from you. Now, let's get on with this. I have a club to run in just a few hours."

"Okay, I'll do it! Just stop!" Marigold yells.

The pain stops, and I turn to look at her.

Her eyes catch mine, and her gaze swims in a sea of sadness.

"It's okay," I mouth. I don't want her to do this. Sure, Marigold has killed people before, but this is an innocent woman. I can read Marigold's expression and see how much this pains her. I don't want her to sacrifice her morality for me. But if I'm killed, Draven can exert this torture on her without even touching her. I'll happily be the scapegoat for her pain.

She nods, tears falling down her cheeks, and stands.

Draven turns to face her, and she gives him an angry look before turning to the woman sitting against the wall. The vampires stand on either side of her, their lifeless expressions staring ahead.

Marigold walks to the unconscious woman, and my heart beats wildly.

"That's it. Just reach out and touch her. That's all you have to do." He brings his drink to his smirking lips.

Marigold's shoulders are shaking as she stands before the frail woman.

I can't stand letting her be so helpless. What good is my power if I can't even use it to protect the person I love most in this world? I want to jump up and intervene, but I stay seated, something in my chest begging me to wait for just a moment more. We can't give up this easily. This can't be the rest of our existence. It just can't.

Draven's laugh sends a chill down my spine as Marigold reaches out her arms and stretches her fingers. I imagine she's trying to take as much time as possible before committing this soul-crushing act. Or maybe she has a plan, just maybe.

It all happens in a flash. She reaches from one guard to the other, turning them into gold statues in mere moments.

We haven't had time to discuss a plan, but I know in an instant that this is my chance. I jump from my seat and snatch my wand off Draven's desk.

Draven is so distracted by the commotion in the corner of his office that he doesn't notice me until the wand is in my hand.

I point my wand at him, but his expression isn't on me. I follow his line of vision to find Marigold suspended in the air, her beautiful face strained in agonizing pain.

"Put the wand down, or I crush Marigold to bits," Draven says in an even tone, keeping his gaze on her.

At first, I don't lower my hand. This will all be for nothing if he kills Marigold. What would he gain by killing her? But I can't risk her life, even for a second.

"Don't do it!" Marigold yells from above us, her veins bulging from the side of her head as if she's using all her might to fight Draven's control.

"I'm sorry." I lower my wand and watch Draven's smirk crawl up his face.

"Change of plans," he says. "It seems having you around is too much of a risk. Besides, I can't think of a better trophy for Marigold and I's first victim together, to be you."

His gaze zooms Marigold through the air and brings her crashing down on top of me. I reach out and grab her as her body falls against mine. Her arms are around my neck, and I hold her close to me with one arm. With the other, I lift my wand again, flicking it at Draven before he can register what happened.

This time, he's the one suspended in the air, his expression strained in pain.

I keep Marigold close to my body, her face buried in my neck.

"How is this possible? You should be gold," Draven says with clenched fists, using all his strength to break free of my power. He may be a powerful wizard and vampire, but I have the upper hand when I have my wand.

"It looks like we don't need your services anymore, but just humor me for a moment. Are you even capable of breaking our curses?"

Draven's eyes are wide and panicked. I imagine he's never met anyone close to his match before. "Yes! Yes, I can break your curses. Your curses must cancel out each other's, but don't you want to be completely curse-free? I can make this possible for you. Hey, Winston, buddy. We can work together. I think Marigold's turned enough of my men into gold. I should be set for a while. Just put me down, and I can completely cure both curses."

I know he's bullshitting me. There's no way that sparing his life would result in a complete change of heart. He's evil. He cares for no one but himself. But even with this thought, I don't know how Marigold feels. Sure, we can touch each other, but her curse affects her so much more than mine. She could have a chance of freedom—to be free of the fear of her curse forever. The curse that makes men want to take advantage of her.

Of course, we aren't virgins anymore, but maybe Draven could possibly have another way to cure us. We obviously defy all odds together. It only makes sense that giving ourselves to each other wouldn't affect the effectiveness of Draven's cure.

I turn to her and search her expression, keeping my wand pointed at Draven.

"Marigold, is it enough for you? Would you be satisfied if I'm the only person you can ever touch?"

Tears cloud her gaze as she searches my face. "Winston, how can you ask me that? Your touch is more than enough. I want you and you alone to touch my skin for the rest of my days." She grabs the back of my neck and pulls her lips to mine.

I taste her want. I know she's not just saying this because she doubts Draven's words. She means it. She wants me and me alone, and of course, I only want her. Of course, being with her is more than enough for me. It's more than I ever dreamed was possible.

I pull back and nod before turning my gaze back to Draven. "Well, it seems that we don't need you after all."

"No!" he screams.

I flick my wand and watch as Draven's neck bends to an unnatural shape. I bring down my wand, and his lifeless body falls to the floor.

Chapter Twenty-Four

MARIGOLD

The low hum of music vibrates my body as I walk into the dark hallway. I feel alive in this place, and although I've been here many times before, the feeling never gets old.

"You look beautiful," Winston whispers before kissing down my neck.

I look down as my dress changes to a bright pink. Of course, I wear this dress to the club every night. It's a magical, morphing, mood-colored dress. Why would a girl need another one?

I've decided to transform it into a short dress with a low back and a swooping neckline for tonight. Winston's hands haven't left my body since I put it on, so I think he's happy with my mental design.

He pulls me against him and runs his hands down my ass, capturing my lips with his.

I lean into him, savoring his sweet taste and allowing my body to melt into him.

A fairy laughs nearby, and I'm knocked out of my trance. I pull back. "We haven't even made it to the lobby."

Winston's heated eyes look down at me, and he shrugs. "This is my club. I can take you anywhere I want." He backs me up to the wall, pressing against me. His hard length rubs against my thigh and sends heat down to my core.

I give a low moan but turn my head. "We're supposed to meet G.M. tonight. I don't want her to find us fucking in the hallway when she arrives."

Winston kisses down my neck and palms at my breasts. "Why not? I'm sure she'd love the show."

I laugh. He's probably right. Although I've been back in the magical community for the last two months and spend every night at Happily Ever Endings with Winston, I still haven't been comfortable enough to have sex in front of others. I imagine that will change soon because God does the thought excite me. I've only been sexually active for a short amount of time. Baby steps.

"Winston," I say in a testing but flirtatious tone.

He gives a heavy breath but then pulls back. "Fine."

I look up at him, suspending himself over me. His hair looks even darker, gelled back, and all I want to do is run my tongue along his clean-shaven jaw, but the night has just started. We can't let into our primal instinct so quickly.

God, you'd think keeping my hands off him would be more bearable after all the sex we've had these past months, but it doesn't get any easier. Our touch is electric. Talk about an addicting sensation.

"God, Marigold. You'll be the death of me." Winston stands, subtly adjusting the bulge in his slacks and keeping his gaze off me as he sucks in deep breaths.

I chuckle and grab his hand, leading him to the club's center, already in full swing.

I wave once I see Liona and Beck seated at the bar, sipping on martinis.

"Marigold!" Liona yells before standing and throwing her arms around me.

My body tenses for a moment, but then I relax once I remember the capabilities of my dress. It will take me a while to get used to the fact that people can touch me with this dress on.

Since we've returned to the magical community, we've told Beck and Liona about our curses. Honestly, it felt good to have someone understand me, and it's nice Liona isn't afraid to embrace me.

Liona pulls back and looks at me. "We've been waiting for you guys. Are you going to watch our show in a little bit?"

My cheeks blush, and I turn back to Winston.

He slips a hand around my waist and pulls me against him. "We're meeting with G.M., so I don't think we'll make it."

This is the real reason, but I'm also still a little uncomfortable with watching my best friends fuck in front of a crowd of people. I know this is just the way of life here, and I have nothing to be embarrassed about, but again, baby steps.

I can't help but notice the look of disappointment on Liona's face, which ignites something strange inside me.

She smiles. "Okay, well, maybe next time."

"Yes, next time," Winston says, looking down to catch my gaze with a small smile.

Liona grabs Beck's hand, and he stands. "Are we still on for this Friday for dinner? I got a babysitter lined up," Liona says as Beck wraps his green arms around her.

"Yes, we'll be there," I reply.

It's nice having friends for once in my life. I love everything about my new life, but most of all, I love the man whose hands are possessively wrapped around my waist right now. I would give it all up just for him.

"See you guys later!" Liona waves to us as she escorts Beck through the crowd to the main stage.

"Winston." A small voice comes from behind us.

We turn toward the nymph receptionist.

"G.M. Fairy has arrived."

***

Winston insists that I sit on his lap during all his meetings. It feels odd to be in such an intimate position while meeting guests, but this is G.M. It's more embarrassing and less embarrassing all at the same time. She's known me since I was a little girl, and now she's watching me as I'm perched on a sex club owner's lap, and he lazily runs his hand up and down my exposed thigh.

Winston didn't give me much of a choice. He hasn't let go of me since we entered his office, and he pulled me on top of him in his chair. When the door opened and G.M. entered, I tried to pull away, but his grip tightened. I complied because I didn't want to make a scene before G.M. I can't say it's the worst position to be in. His erection presses against my ass, and his touch sends tingles to my core. I don't think I'll ever get used to the surge of electricity that pulses between our touch. I love the feeling of him, but God, is this a lot to handle.

His smirk hasn't left his face, so I imagine he senses my discomfort and is enjoying it.

"Well, it seems the trip to Draven worked. You two seem awfully close," G.M. smiles as she crosses her legs in the wingback chair in front of Winston's desk.

"Not quite." Winston's expression turns serious. "Draven was a fraud."

G.M. frowns. "Then how..."

I speak up. "Our curses counteract or cancel each other. We're not sure if it's because our curses are from the same witch or if it's in the wording of the curses themself, but we had to escape near death to discover it."

G.M.'s expression turns grave. "Near death? What happened?"

"Did you know Draven was evil?" Winston's voice is so gruff and stern that it catches me off guard.

G.M.'s expression morphs into confusion. "No! I knew he was a cocky jackass that ran a less-than-desirable club. We'd gotten into it a few times during the magical council meetings regarding the safety of humans. I knew he wasn't fond of me, but I've never heard of him doing anything purely evil to anyone in the magical community."

I've known G.M. my whole life. Of course, I believe her. I turn to catch Winston's steeled gaze and grab his wrist.

He looks down at me and studies my expression.

I plead with my eyes for him to lighten up. I know he's still shaken up from the messiness with Draven, but this is G.M. Fairy we're talking about. She didn't know what she was sending us to. I don't even have to hear her explanation to know that.

Finally, he breathes out, and his shoulders relax. He nods at me and returns his attention to G.M. "Okay, I believe you. We don't have to worry about him anymore. I killed him."

G.M. shakes her head. "I'm so sorry that I put you both through this. I thought this was Marigold's only hope. I guess when you're desperate, you fail to see hidden dangers."

I know what she means. We all should have been more cautious when planning to meet with Draven, but we just wanted our curses to be broken so badly that we were willing to risk it all.

"It's okay," I say, leaning over the desk to clasp her hand. "I know you didn't know." I catch her gaze in mine.

Tears form behind her small glasses, and she gives me a soft smile. "I'm just so glad to see you happy, Marigold. It was never about your curse being broken. Since the day you were born, all I wanted was for you to be loved on a deeper level."

Even though G.M. never showed me much affection growing up, she has always been a mother figure to me. My heart overflows to see her happy for me.

"Thank you, G.M." I squeeze her hand one last time before resting against Winston. I lean against his chest and gaze up at him. "I am truly loved."

"I should have known." G.M. sighs.

I turn back to catch G.M. staring at us and shaking her head. "I should have known you two were meant to break each other's curses. I felt it the moment you two caught sight of each other. It's like the air around you both ignite with magic. Your each other's destiny."

"I guess I should thank you," Winston says, his gaze still on me. "If you didn't bring us together, I'd live my whole life without knowing this bliss. I'd do it all over again. I'd go through hell and back to hold Marigold in my arms."

My cheeks heat at his words. He's always had a way with words, but it does something extra special when he's proclaiming his love in front of others.

G.M. is right. We all should have known we were destined for each other the moment we met. Of course, I knew it the second I saw him. I only wish I admitted it to myself sooner.

"Well, I'm happy for you both." G.M. rises from her chair. "I think I know when a room should be cleared out for lovers, so I'll see my way out. Besides, I have a show to catch." She gives us a wink before fluttering to the door.

The second the door shuts behind G.M., Winston's lips are against my neck. "God, I thought she'd never leave."

"Winston," I scold, already out of breath from his touch.

"I just need you, Marigold. I couldn't wait another second."

I pick myself up and turn to straddle him. "But you just had me at home. Isn't that enough?" I slowly grind against him, my dress rides up my ass, and he grabs me, pulling me against him.

"Haven't you learned anything in the past few months? I can never get enough of you. I dream of your scent, your touch, your taste." He grabs my neck and pulls me against his lips.

He pulls back and whispers in my ear. "It will never be enough, Marigold. We have a lifetime to explore every part of each other, and by the gods, I promise you, I will be as greedy as the first time we touched until the last."

"Winston," is all I manage to get out breathlessly. I've never been good with words, but I hope he can feel the love I have for him seep out of me.

We're not in his chair anymore. I open my eyes to find us floating above his office. We're weightless, suspended in the air by magic, free to explore each other without any limitations.

Winston pushes my dress down, and it falls to the floor below us.

I work on unbuttoning his shirt as he slips out of his slacks and boxers.

My hands get lost in his mess of hair as he explores my breasts, my ass, the heat between my legs.

I don't let him explore much, though. An urgency to have him deep inside of me overwhelms me. I want him to see just how much I need him—how much he completes me. I crawl down his body, grabbing his cock and positioning at my entrance.

Although he loves to make me come before he penetrates me, he's no match for my needs. I impale myself with him, and his moans echo throughout the office.

"Marigold," he moans, grabbing me as if I might slip away. He thrusts in and out of me slowly but with an undeniable need. He hits me so deep that my moans strangle in the back of my throat.

This isn't going to last long. We're both so hungry for each other that we can't control ourselves. It's okay, though. If tonight is anything like every night since I moved into Winston's cottage for the past two months, it won't be the last time we're tangled together.

My vision blurs as Winston pumps deeper and faster. My orgasm rises from my toes, and my whole body turns into a sputtering mess in a matter of seconds.

He releases himself inside me at the same time I come to my crescendo. I milk him for every last drop as he slowly lowers us back to his chair, sending kisses from my cheek down my neck.

I sigh and nuzzle against him, still eager for every bit of him.

"My Marigold," he sighs as he tucks a strand of hair behind my ear. "You are magic."

"We're magic," I correct, still keeping my eyes closed.

He leans down and kisses my forehead. His soft kiss sends a rush of electricity down my body.

It's now dawning on me—-the secret to our curses. We aren't mere mortals. Our electric touch, our ability to make love in the heavens, it all just proves to me that our love is otherworldly.

I'm a girl with a golden touch, and he's a boy who can never be touched, but together, we aren't cursed. Together, we're gods.

THANKS FOR READING

Thank you for reading! If you liked *Spellbound Seduction: A Wizard Love Story*, please make sure to leave a review on Amazon and Goodreads.

Want more of G.M. Fairy? Check out her other books...

My AI: A Robot Why-Choose Love Story

After social media star Azzy, has a very public panic attack at a red-carpeted award show, her best friend orders her an Andro Corp. Bodyguard. When her robot bodyguard gets delivered, Azzy quickly realizes Model REM082 is the man of her dreams. Things start heating up as Remmy, as she likes to call him, becomes more and more sentient and does whatever it takes to please her.

Get In My Swamp: An Ogre Love Story

Book 1: When Liona stumbles upon Beck, the ogre's, trap and becomes his prisoner, she's determined to get away. But it doesn't take long for things to start heating up between the two. Beck is trying to protect her, and Liona can't help her body's reaction to the buff green monster. The lines between captive and captor become blurry, and the passion becomes a raging fire neither of them can put out.

Stay In My Swamp: An Ogre Happily Ever After

Book 2: Life in the swamp can't get any better for Liona and Beck. That's until Beck pops a big question that forces Liona to face some unfinished business. She heads back to LA but Beck isn't too far behind, this time looking less like an ogre thanks to some help from Winston the Wizard. Will magic be enough for Beck to get Liona to stay in his swamp forever?

Stay up to date on all things G.M. Fairy!

Made in the USA
Monee, IL
01 December 2024

71769913R00090